Alison's Gift

The Song of a Thousand Hearts Opening

PAT HOGAN

NOSILA Publishing
Silver Spring, Maryland

ISBN: 0-9668177-0-2
LCCN: 98-92216

Printed in the United States of America

This book was printed on acid-free paper and with environmental considerations in mind.

Book Production: Phelps & Associates

Publisher's Cataloging-in-Publication
(Provided by Quality Books, Inc.)

Hogan, Pat (Patrick Joseph), 1957–
    Alison's gift : the song of a thousand hearts
    opening / Pat Hogan. -- 1st ed.
    p. cm.
    LCCN: 98-92216
    ISBN: 0-9668177-0-2

    1. Death--Religious aspects--Christianity.
    2. Bereavement--Religious aspects--Christianity.
    3. Sanders, Alison, 1988–1995--Death and burial.
    4. Traffic accident victims. 5. Air bag restraint
    systems. I. Title

BT825.H64 1999   236.1
                            QBI98-1551

She was here today
Kissing you with sunshine
And running wind fingers through your hair

Tonight she'll tuck you in
Under a blanket of clouds
And keep quiet sentry while you sleep

A breath of wind
A rustle of leaves
The chirp of crickets
The tick of a clock

And in the morning
She'll tickle you with dappled sunlight
To waken you to a new day

– Lurana

table of contents

PREFACE: Crossings vii

CHAPTER ONE: Between Life and Death 1

CHAPTER TWO: Ground Zero 23

CHAPTER THREE: Spirit in the Night 47

CHAPTER FOUR: Where the Heart Is 57

CHAPTER FIVE: Touching the Light 71

CHAPTER SIX: Show Time 81

CHAPTER SEVEN: Out of the Depths 99

CHAPTER EIGHT: Aftermath and Going On 109

CHAPTER NINE: Anniversaries and Co-inkydinks 121

CHAPTER TEN: Legacies and Silver Linings 127

EPILOGUE: Rites and Rituals for Renewal 139

APPENDIX A: Crossings Care 143

APPENDIX B: Frequently Asked Questions 149

ENDNOTES 151

preface

CROSSINGS

Have you ever seen a squirrel cross the road? Squirrels in their thick gray camouflaged skins usually dart across the road. When a car approaches, they react quickly. If a squirrel is by the side of the road, it will turn in lightning motion and scurry to safety. Squirrels are unmasked against the open street and millions of years of evolution have not prepared them for a hurtling two-ton vehicle. Usually they freeze for an instant. In the blink of an eye they turn toward what had been safety, wondering whether to return in that direction. Usually they will dart to a side of the road — and escape to deal with other dangerous, but understood, acts of nature.

Sometimes it is not clear which path to take. Squirrels move left, then right, then left. They dance the dance of nakedness, seeking inspiration for a way out. Their dance is a spastic ballet of reflex gyrations with a mad dash at the last instant. Usually the car and the squirrel pass without contact and the dance fulfills its purpose. Sometimes not.

We too are faced with many road crossings that bring unforeseen danger. There is a vehicle — of karma, of God, of evil — bearing down on us, an uninvited disruptive presence. We run for cover at the first scent of danger, wishing to return to our regularly scheduled lives. We look back upon the mundane with idyllic longing.

Sometimes the side of the road we came from is torn from us like the cold fall wind whips leaves from trees. Sometimes the other side is too far to reach. We freeze. We turn quickly. We do our voodoo dance of denial and hope, praying that we will be spared, asking for guidance, hoping to be released. Oftentimes this dance of superstitious ignorance sees us through without harm. We flirt with near catastrophe, prolonged suffering, even death, and come away to live another day. Sometimes not.

The dance is a dance of revelation. Our hopes, passions, pains, and joys are revealed. We dance an awkward, primal dance of graceless stilted movement — a dance beyond the rituals and procedures for protecting us, a dance that joins us with our destiny. We watch ourselves, wishing to get past, while we have in fact come forth to meet this vehicle of destruction and transformation.

Usually we come away intact. At times we are changed forever. This, however, is a call that must be answered. It is the call of our spirit on a well-traveled path often hidden from sight.

Gradually we learn this dance and flow with unique purposefulness and grace. We are grateful for our growth and welcome this invitation. We embrace our lives and dance forth inspired.

between life and death

SUNDAY, OCTOBER 15, 1995

Beth was waving frantically from the door. She was a silhouette in the growing darkness, a cordless phone in her hand. We had just spent an enjoyable weekend together. I was warming up my car preparing to leave and could hear nothing over the rumble of the engine. The evening darkness was nearly complete and the soft warmth of the early autumn night had given way to a coolness in the air. Turning off the engine, I hurried to the house.

"There's been an accident!" Beth said. "And they're taking Alison to the hospital. Here!" she said handing me the phone.

I took the phone and studied it a long moment. Was she handing me the phone to emphasize her statement, or was there someone on the line?

"Speak!!" she shouted pointing at the phone.

"Hello. Can I help you?" I said.

Beth was breathing quickly now, nearly hyperventilating. She gave out a stifled moan.

"If anything has happened..." Beth said.

I took the phone into the kitchen away from her.

"Hello! Yes," a woman's voice replied, "this is Ms. —— from Sinai Hospital. There's been an automobile accident involving Alison Sanders and they are trying to save her right now."

"How do we get there?" I said grabbing a pen and paper. She gave me directions coming from the Washington, D.C. suburbs: up I-95 into Baltimore, then onto I-83, the hospital exit would be marked. Thanking her, I hung up the phone and had turned to Beth when the phone rang.

"Hello."

"Pat this is Lyn," an agitated voice started. It was Lyn Post, the children's stepmother. (Alison, 7, David, 9, and Matthew, 10, had spent the weekend in Baltimore with Beth's former husband Rob Sanders, Lyn, and their new baby, Lindsey.) "There's been an accident—"

"Yes, I know. We just got a call from the hospital."

"They're trying to revive Alison and I'm heading over to the hospital to join Rob."

"We're jumping in the car," I said. "We'll be there as soon as we can."

Beth broke in, "Where are the boys?"

Lyn heard Beth's question through the phone.

"The boys are here," Lyn told me. "They are both fine, and they can stay with my sister who is here for the weekend." I told Beth the boys were fine and that Lyn's sister, Laurie, would stay with them.

"Lyn, we're on our way," I said. "We'll see you there."

Beth grabbed her jacket and the waist pack that she uses as a purse. I threw on my long sleeve shirt. I was relieved to be able to take some action, and we hurried to leave the house. Beth's cat, Pumpkin, an orange tabby, was around our feet as we got out the door.

I decided we should take my car instead of Beth's van. It was nearly an hour's drive to the hospital, and my car would hold the road better. I restarted the car and the muffler gave its distinctive rumble. I kept our speed at 70 mph on the highway; this was over the limit but not excessive. After all, we were not sure where things stood: Alison was in the hospital being revived, Rob was with her, and the boys were back at Lyn's.

As we drove up I-95 to Baltimore, Beth became more composed. She was praying and focusing on the strength of her relationship to her little girl. This internal focus helped calm her down. The drive was monotonous, and the drone of the engine had a soothing effect.

I began to have my own thoughts, searching within myself to feel that wonderful connection that I had with Alison. Could I sense how she was doing? No clear feelings arose. I believed that she was not crying out for help or suffering greatly. The alternatives, I recognized, were either that she had been through a frightening experience and was relatively uninjured, or that she had died and passed on from this life. I tried to determine which of these seemed most likely, but my feelings told me nothing. The miles went by slowly in what seemed an incredibly long journey — my headlights, like my feelings, illuminating little in the darkness around me.

As we approached the city, I began to formulate something I felt I had to say before we reached the hospital. We got into Baltimore and wound our way through downtown until we reached the entrance ramp for I-83. Back on an expressway, we were nearing the hospital. I picked through my thoughts until I garnered the most benign expression possible. I could put it off no longer.

"Beth," I said, "when Lyn called, she said that they were working to revive Alison."

A deep silence fell as Beth sorted through my words and her feelings. There was silence.

Silence.

"So," Beth finally said, "she may be dead."

"Yes, she may be dead," my hollow words echoed.

Silence.

We had spoken the words that comprehended the incomprehensible.

Two Years Earlier

Beth and I first met a dozen years earlier when she was in her late twenties. She was married to Rob at the time and I knew them both casually. Rob and I played touch football on Sunday mornings, and Beth had come out to see him play. They had started to raise a family and I occasionally saw one or both of them. I lost track of them over the years before Beth and I met again.

Interestingly, this happened through the "personals" of the local paper. I placed an ad, and Beth responded under the name "Elizabeth." When I called her back, she introduced herself as Elizabeth. Because of my phone sales training I gave my full name, "Hi, this is Pat Hogan."

We talked for a few minutes and then Beth said that she did not think this would work; she thought she knew who I was. I asked her to describe me and she did — accurately.

"Maybe we should let this one go," she said, "but if you would like to keep talking, I may feel more comfortable about letting you know who I am."

What was I to do? She had me at a disadvantage and I was quite curious to know who "Elizabeth" was. So we talked and laughed about different things and occasionally I would try to guess who she was. The anonymity gave us the opportunity to share ourselves in a way that was lively and fun.

Eventually I figured out who she was. She was talking, and I broke in, "Okay, okay, I've got it!" I said, "I know who you are. Now it's *your* turn to squirm!"

We both had a good laugh, and I enjoyed our conversation immensely. I found that Beth lived only a half mile from me so we decided to get together for tea that evening. We went dancing the next weekend and began spending time together.

Beth and Rob were not divorced at that time although they had been separated for four years. Soon thereafter, Rob became engaged to Lyn, and he and Beth moved to complete matters between them. Beth had been rebuilding her life. It had been a long haul of recognizing self-worth and working through difficulties, but most of that was behind her and she was ready to move ahead.

I met Alison for the first time when I saw Beth at the local supermarket. Beth introduced me to her as a "friend." Alison was sitting in the grocery cart, a cute five-year-old girl with full hazel eyes and light brown hair. She was quiet and did not make a strong impression on me.

For a time after Beth and I were together, I would come over to Beth's for a visit after the children had gone to bed. Beth wanted to keep our relationship between ourselves, and we both thought that involving the children was a step to take after some time had passed. When Alison finally found out that I had been coming by in the evenings, she said that she had often heard a "gruff voice" downstairs.

One day I came over and Alison and I had a chance to get acquainted. As she gravitated to men, men gravitated to Alison. At one point I picked her up and tossed her over my back and swung her in circles, giving her a thrill and myself a workout. Before putting her back on her feet, I raised her over my head and dropped her, letting her fall nearly to the floor.

"Pat, you're awesome!" she exclaimed. We had both found a friend.

Eventually, Rob and I met again. We had good feelings toward each other from our past association. I also cared for the children, and I believe that Rob felt my presence was positive.

ARRIVING AT SINAI HOSPITAL

Beth and I were still dressed in our shorts from the warm day when we arrived at the hospital. I dropped Beth off at the emergency room entrance and parked the car. Once inside, I asked for Alison.

An intern kindly took me upstairs. We made small talk; then I tried to find out what I could from him. There was nothing he could tell me.

"I guess," I surmised, "it's a positive sign that they're still with her and working on her, that she has gotten this far."

"Well," he said in a noncommittal way, "that's not always the case."

The door opened and he led me down a hall to the imaging area where Alison was having a CAT scan done on her. Beth, wearing a shielded apron, was by her side. (When Beth had arrived, she immediately wanted to be with Alison, but was informed that her daughter was having a CAT scan done, and she should wait for that to be completed. With calm determination, Beth asked for a lead apron so that she could join her daughter. One was found without delay, and she joined Alison in the imaging room.)

I was told to go to the waiting room, where I stayed for some time without seeing anyone. I ventured into the hall to see if I could wait by the area where they were doing the imaging. A group was gathered around the control panel of the instrument.

A doctor saw me, "Who are you?"

I tried to think what my true relationship to Alison was. Friend? No clout there. I came up with what I felt was most deeply true.

"I'm her godfather," I said.

He waved me off dismissively. "Please go back to the waiting room."

"Okay," I thought to myself, "next time I'm her uncle!"

Fifteen minutes later the doctor who had been working on Alison came in. He had worked a long shift, but there was a deeper tiredness in his eyes. He told me that they were still running tests on Alison and that she was being taken to another hospital, but that things did not look good. That seemed confusing. She was breathing, they were still working on her, and they were sending her to a better facility; yet, things "did not look good."

I stayed in the waiting room, and Beth walked in shortly afterwards.

"They want to take her over to Johns Hopkins Hospital," she said. "It's the central pediatric unit for the area and they feel that it will be best for Alison. I'm going to ride over in the ambulance with her."

"That sounds good!" I said.

Beth asked me if I would check on the boys at Lyn's house, and then she returned to be with Alison. Lyn, Rob's wife, came around the corner and was quite upset.

"I've been downstairs with Rob," she said. "He's beside himself and nearly out of control. Is there any progress?"

I shared what I knew and told her I would stop by her house before going downtown to Johns Hopkins. I asked Lyn what had happened in the accident. She explained that Rob was bringing the children home after dinner and had collided with another vehicle less than two miles from their home. Rob had called Lyn from the hospital.

Beth came back around the corner to tell me that they were preparing to leave.

"How is Alison?" Lyn asked.

"She's on a ventilator that is breathing for her."

"Oh God! I'm so sorry!" Lyn said. "Rob is very distressed, and they want to medicate him. He's down in the emergency room, but he won't take anything." She turned to me, "Pat, maybe you could say something to Rob before you leave."

Lyn gave me directions to her house. Beth gave me the phone numbers for family, friends, and the children's teachers to contact once I got to Lyn's house. Lyn, who had started down the stairs to rejoin Rob, hurried back to us and went straight to Beth.

"I just wanted to say —" she choked up.

There was nothing to say. The two mothers held each other for a moment — a long moment — then Lyn turned and walked past me in tears as both women returned to their loved ones.

I went downstairs and on my way through the emergency room saw Rob. He had a wild look in his eyes, and he latched onto me like a drowning man adrift at sea. A large guard hovered near him.

"Pat! How is she?" he said in a raspy, pained voice.

"They're sending her to Johns Hopkins," I said, trying to console him.

"How is she doing?" he was distracted, near despair.

"Well, she's breathing," I said. (I did not say that she was on a ventilator.)

"Oh...she's breathing for herself now," he said distractedly.

I did not correct him. It sounded good — too good to contradict. They were still trying to calm Rob as I left.

I later learned from Lyn that when Beth came downstairs on her way to the ambulance she saw Rob and went over to him. She was composed. They talked for a few minutes and Beth said positive things about Alison and expressed hope that she would pull through. At the same time, she recognized the possibility that this would not happen. Lyn told me that Beth had spoken lovingly to Rob and had not blamed him. She had even told Rob that if this was all they had of Alison in their lives that it had been a great blessing, and if Alison was no longer to be with them that her life had been an incredible gift.

Lyn said, "Beth spoke with love in her heart. There was no blame or hatred. She tried to uplift Rob even though she was facing the possible loss of her daughter. I don't know how she did it." Pausing for a moment, Lyn said, "I could not have done what Beth did."

A NIGHTMARE — ONE MONTH EARLIER

Thump! Thrash! Beth shot up in bed.

"What is it?" I asked. Beth was shaken.

"I just had a nightmare. It was one of the children. I saw a face at the morgue." She started to cry. "Pat, I don't know what I'd do! They'll be all right, won't they? They're the most precious thing in the world to me." She grabbed a tissue and blew her nose.

"I'm going upstairs to check on them," she said. Beth went upstairs in the dark to the children.

I sat in the blackness thinking, "Don't all parents go through this? Isn't this normal?" Beneath these thoughts I knew that life was inherently uncertain.

Upstairs, Beth kissed the children and checked on each of them, stroking their peaceful sleeping forms. She knelt down by their beds and prayed, imploring a just and merciful God to protect and care for the family and to watch over her children. She spent time with each child, and when she came downstairs appeared to be more at ease. Still, she had had several nightmares like this in the last few months, and that was disturbing.

Were these dreams a reflection of the struggles and triumphs of daily living, or were they a deeper indicator of the flow of life beyond her sight? Regardless, that night the children slept soundly in safety and security. Beth had done all she could do, the rest was in God's hands.

ON CALL

Although I had been to Lyn and Rob's house several times before, and it was not far from the hospital, I still got lost. I ended up driving around for some time and was getting frustrated when, out of nowhere, I came upon it.

At Lyn's house I met Laurie, Lyn's sister, and her children, Eli, 13, and Emily, 8. All of the children, including Matthew and David, were watching baseball playoffs. Matthew and David were two blond and bright children. They were different in their attitudes and capabilities, yet they complemented each other well. I had a good relationship with the boys, who were separated by just seventeen months, and we had shared some wonderful experiences and many outings together. We exchanged hellos and I gave them an update on Alison's condition. The children had been told that Alison was unconscious as a result of the accident, and I informed them that nothing had changed.

Laurie and I spoke in the kitchen, and she told me what she knew of the accident. Apparently, as Rob was driving the children home, one of the boys asked if they could hear the Washington Redskins football game on the radio. When Rob pressed the button for the station, nothing happened. He looked down and tried to fix the problem. When he looked up, the light at the intersection they were approaching had changed. Rob put on the brakes, but his car entered the intersection at about 10 mph and collided into the side of a vehicle. Alison was the only one injured.

After our conversation, I started calling from the list that Beth had given me. First I called the children's teachers to let them know that they would not be at school the next day. Then I called members of Beth's family, all of whom lived out of town: her mother, Faith Knox, her sister, Kay Knox, and her cousin, Charity Turner. I also called her close friends, Jane Parker and Soraya Howard. I was unable to reach another friend, Camilla Lake.

When I called Beth's mother, her answering machine was on.

"Great," I thought, "she's already gone to bed, and I missed her."

I then called Beth's sister, Kay, who said that she would try to reach their mother.

When I called Jane, I told her that Beth wanted her to come to the hospital. Jane told me that her husband was working through the night and probably would not be back to stay with their children.

"If I can reach him, and he is able to come home, then I may be able to come, but I'm not sure," Jane said. I did not expect to see her.

Beth's cousin Charity reacted strongly. She kept saying, "Oh God! Oh God!" and was shaken by the news.

Faith called me after Beth's sister reached her. I told her what I knew about her granddaughter's condition: there had been an accident, Alison was in the hospital, she had had a CAT scan and was now being transferred to Johns Hopkins Hospital, she was on a ventilator, and her heart was beating. I told her that I would keep her posted.

Beth called from Johns Hopkins. They had arrived and a medical team was working on Alison.

"How are the boys?" she asked.

"They're fine."

"Tell them to pray for Alison. Tell them I love them."

By this time the children were already asleep, but I went to each one.

"Your mom called from the hospital." I told David. "She is still with Alison"

"Did Alison wake up yet?"

"No, Sweetie, she has not. She needs our prayers."

David rolled over and sat up, folding his hands together. We said a quick prayer and immediately he dozed off again. I woke Matthew and passed on the same information. He was more alert.

"Where's Daddy?"

"Daddy is still at the hospital with Lyn and your mom."

We prayed that Alison would be fine and that God would take care of her. I passed on Beth's love and then got back on the phone.

I kept talking and updating, taking phone calls, switching back and forth on call-waiting as information and concern buzzed back and forth across the miles. Kay had also contacted her father, John Knox, and informed him of the news. In a way, the busy work was a relief: being in contact with family and friends felt good, and their concern and support were helpful.

LESSONS IN SHARING: A MEMORY

"Alison, why don't you pick first?"

I had known Alison a short time and she and I were dividing up six small treats. There were two that looked better than the others. Alison picked both of these.

"Alison," I said, "just pick one at a time."

Obviously, this was going to be a lesson in fair play for her. I did not mind her getting both of the better items, I just wanted it done fairly. She put one back, and then I took one of the other treats allowing her to pick the better treat for herself. Instead she picked one of the other treats. I chose again, still leaving her the remaining better item. She did the same, forcing me to have the last and better treat.

As a child, I expected Alison to be motivated by her needs and to take the other good treat. Instead she made sure I got it. I was going to instruct her in fairness, and she showed me that harmony was more important. She wanted her relationships to be win-win

11

and worked to create that. Where I had come to teach, I found myself the student.

It was a small event, and it almost slipped by unnoticed. I was certain of a particular outcome, instead a depth of character was revealed. I would come to see this as the norm rather than the exception with Alison: she had the body of a child but the heart and soul of a much wiser being.

AT JOHNS HOPKINS HOSPITAL

I eventually left Lyn's house after midnight. Finding my way to Johns Hopkins Hospital Center was not difficult considering the fact that I didn't know my way around Baltimore. I only had to ask for directions once.

Johns Hopkins Hospital Center is in one of the worst areas of the city. Dilapidated buildings are everywhere in this inner city neighborhood. Rising up by itself is a large, well-kept medical complex of thirty-odd buildings and parking garages, some built into each other or over one another. They are strung together by a network of bridges and underground tunnels. It is a large vibrant being in the heart of the inner city. It also employs a small army of security guards to deal with the neighborhood.

I found a parking garage and saw people coming out of the hospital. They directed me inside, where I came to the front desk.

I was in a hurry. Beth had asked me to join her in our last phone conversation, and I had been gone for hours. The nurses had encouraged her to call someone to be with her. Although she was quite content being alone with Alison, she thought that they knew best and had asked me to join her. It was now about 1 A.M. When I got to the front desk, I showed my ID and told the guard that I was with the Sanders family.

"But you are not a family member!" the guard retorted.

I was upset and let him know it. I told him that they were waiting on me and that a little girl was in serious condition. The guard made a call, and then gave me the okay. He found an escort to make sure it was all right for me to be on the ward. We wound our way through the passages of Johns Hopkins to the elevators for the pediatric intensive care unit. Soon this labyrinth of hallways and passages would be all too familiar.

Upstairs, Rob and Lyn were in a small private sitting room off of the hall. This room had a love seat, two chairs, a small table, and a phone. Beth was across the hall with Alison. I exchanged updates with Rob and Lyn. Alison's father looked haggard and had a white blanket draped over him. There was still no determination of Alison's condition. I left to join Alison and Beth.

Alison was in a large room divided into two groups of four beds. I took in the room just before I entered: all of these children struggling for life in critical care! Alison's bed was in a corner near a window. I felt some trepidation as I walked in because I been talking with friends and family about Alison for hours, yet I had not seen her. I was also unsure how Beth was feeling and did not wish to intrude on her if she wanted privacy.

Approaching Alison's bed, I joined Beth. I was struck by Alison's eyes. They were half open and had a clear liquid in them to keep them from drying out. Although her eyes were open, she was not conscious. At regular intervals her chest would rise and fall with the support of the assisted breathing unit, the ventilator, next to her bed.

Beth mothered and stroked her daughter, talking to her, kissing her, and loving her in many ways. Beth was happy to see me and said that they were continuing to do tests on Alison. Alison was hooked up to several IVs, an EKG machine, and a blood pressure unit. She was wearing a large neck brace that had been put on at the scene of the accident. There was also a rash-type mark on her neck. It was more like a scrape and was red. It was hidden under the brace for the most part. Her lips were bruised. Although I had been telling people about Alison for hours, her condition was different than what I had pictured. How was she really?

Peggy was our nurse. She divided her time between a few other children and Alison. She was competent and served Alison and Beth well. I got Beth some water and comforted her, also stroking Alison and holding her hand. Time went by with Peggy checking in on us often. There was no definitive statement of Alison's condition or prognosis.

Over the course of our stay we got to know the three nurses assigned to Alison at different shifts. They were all professional, caring, and competent. As I chatted with Peggy, I told her that I had had trouble getting up to the ward. She expressed concern for our welfare as well as Alison's and that was comforting.

Rob came in and out of the room, briefly visiting with Alison and talking to her. It was obvious he felt enormous anguish and responsibility over what had happened to his little girl. He was distraught and grabbed every nurse and doctor available trying to get answers. No one knew anything beyond what we had already been told. Several times doctors needed to see Alison privately and everyone was asked to leave the room. Time was going by, but there was little change.

Suddenly, a bright blue angel appeared before me. It was Jane, Beth's close friend, with a slightly wry smile. She was wearing blue jeans and a blue jean jacket. She was tall and striking. She said she did not think she could come, and yet here she was! I was thrilled for her support and steadiness.

Rob was overwhelmed, Lyn was taking care of him, and Beth was occupied with Alison. In Jane the right person had come. She was physically and emotionally strong and willing to take on any task. There was a feeling of strength now. Jane and I could parcel out responsibilities and I knew things would go well.

Jane had driven up to Baltimore into the full moon from the Washington, D.C. suburbs. As she drove, she had prayed for Alison and thought of her. Alison's presence seemed to be in the moon and Jane felt that it had guided her safely in the late night to the hospital. She found street parking in the dilapidated area near the hospital and a security guard came by. She latched on to him and had him deliver her to the front door. She had brought a beautiful quilt from her home for Alison's hospital bed, and it made a nice difference in how the room felt. Jane had come to give of herself and her help was needed.

SEPTEMBER, 1995

"Alison, it's time for bed. Boys, please quiet down in there."

Beth was getting the children settled and into bed. Alison was sleeping in her room now. For several years she had slept in the window seat in the upstairs hallway. It made a nice little cubby for her, and when she had outgrown that, she had moved to the love seat in the boy's room. She loved to be around others and this was a natural place for her. Only when she had outgrown the love seat, did she finally use her room for sleeping.

Alison was in the Washington Waldorf School, a private school that started children in classes at a later age than public schools. She was seven years old and finally in first grade. She was thrilled! At last, she was a "big first grader" and was looked upon lovingly and with respect by classmates and teachers. She had been one of the oldest children in kindergarten the year before and here she was — a real student! The experience was all that she had hoped, and in her first month of school new horizons were opening up before her.

Evenings were often difficult for Alison though. She found it hard to get to sleep. In fact, Alison sometimes commented that she had not slept at all during the night. This was not true, of course. She slept deeply, but somehow there was a wakefulness that pierced through even her deepest sleep.

The transition from the activities of the day to the quiet of the evening brought an introspective quality. This was a time Beth and Alison enjoyed, sharing thoughts and reflections of the day, before Alison (slowly!) drifted off to sleep. As often happened, Beth and Alison talked about school and friends and simple things of importance that they both shared.

"All right, Alison. It's time to settle down and get some sleep. I love you!"

"I love you, Momma." There was a pause.

"Momma," Alison looked up with her sweet but firm gaze, "I'll always be with you."

Beth looked intently at Alison thinking, "Yes, Alison, when I'm gone you'll always be with me." Such a wise and loving child!

"And I'll always be with you, too," she said. They kissed.

"Good night, Momma."

"Good night, Sweetheart."

LATE AT NIGHT

After the accident, I found myself looking back on the day that Beth and I had spent together. Were there any clues or signs to the unusual events to follow?

We had awakened to a gorgeous morning, that Sunday in mid-October. There was not a cloud in the sky and we dressed in shorts for the warm fall day. I thought that we should go out for brunch and called my parents for advice on a nice restaurant. My mother invited us to their house where my sister's family and her in-laws were joining them for brunch. Beth and I accepted and we enjoyed a wonderful meal with terrific company. We had our bikes and afterwards we went exploring in a forested park nearby. We stopped off to see friends in the evening, enjoyed a nice dinner, and then returned to Beth's house just after sunset, which is when the hospital called.

When I looked over the day and our activities, I could only be filled with the gladness of a day well spent. Nowhere in the day could I find a rough edge or doubt. The day was filled with those things that Beth and I treasure: love, family, friends, food, natural beauty, and bliss. It was not a unique day, but it was deeply satisfying.

My reflections convinced me that there was nothing we should have done differently that day. We had been given the opportunity to live fully and we had done so. We had been given blessings, and we had shared them in many ways in many places with many people. It is not possible to be everywhere at once, but if you live fully where you are, I believe that all life benefits.

Ultimately, this exercise brought with it the understanding that the coming events were not just an "accident." This was a source of comfort in the confusion that Beth and I experienced. It gave us faith in the process at hand.

Conversely, however, Beth had been less active than usual over the weekend. She had shied away from activities in which she normally engaged. She was more introspective. On a subtle level, it seemed now, her life forces were being marshalled. Things had not been quite right with Beth, but there was nothing identifiably wrong.

We were hoping and praying that we would get Alison back. We prayed that she would return to consciousness and come through this situation. Knowing the Alison with boundless energy, exuberance, and joy, it was hard relating to this little girl with the ventilator breathing for her.

As time passed, Beth became upset with herself. She told me that she could not remember saying good-bye to Alison on Friday night when the children had left with Rob.

Rob had come by as he always did to pick up the children for the weekend. He had just replaced his older car with a new minivan that he thought would be safer for the whole family. Alison had gone out to the car early. The children took turns having the front seat with Daddy. Alison got the front seat Friday night as well as Sunday evening for the ride home.

I had arrived just as the children and Rob were preparing to leave and found the house in its usual state of disarray at those times. I remember Alison standing by the fireplace in the living room when I came in. The children were always preoccupied when Rob showed up at the end of the week. It was as though they had been reunited after a long and difficult separation, like a magnet that finally comes close enough to exert its pull and is instantaneously joined by the attraction. Beth and I went to the door as Rob and the boys got into the minivan. They drove off and we waved to everyone. I could not see Alison, but I felt her joyful presence in the farewell.

Beth remembered saying good-bye to the boys but could not remember what had happened with Alison. This was disturbing to her, because she had always made a conscious effort to ensure her partings with the children were loving. And here Alison was, unconscious before her, and she could not remember a hug and a kiss good-bye. Alison also hated good-byes, and it was strange that on this weekend, of all times, that there had been none.

Over the weekend, Alison did call home once. Alison called, as she often did, on behalf of the children. This time she asked for permission to go to a movie. Sometimes she would call to ask if the children could do something special or ask Beth for a ruling on a new activity. She would even call when they were doing something that they were not supposed to do, such as watching more TV or movies than were allowed. Although the youngest, Alison was the conscience of the group, and when she agreed to a set of rules, she took that responsibility seriously.

Beth was home when Alison called, and they had a nice talk at the end of which they both said, "I love you." This was the last contact Beth had with Alison before the accident. Still, she was not able to remember Alison leaving on Friday night. It left an indelible mark on Beth regarding her awareness of her children and treating every parting with the sanctity it deserves.

BEACH NOTE, AUGUST 1995

We had gone to the beach at the end of the summer. One evening I came upstairs, and Alison handed me a piece of paper.

"I made this for you," she said.

It was a plain piece of off-white drawing paper that had been folded into quarters. On the outside it read "Pat," and on the inside it read, "I love you — from Alison."

She also had made one for her Aunt Kay and we compared them. The notes were identical except Kay's read, "I lov you." Kay and I joked about the misspelling, and Alison asked what was so funny. We explained that her mistake was quite endearing and that we enjoyed her efforts.

Alison looked up at me seriously and said, "I want you to keep this."

I told her that I would, convinced at the time that I was doing so for her sake, not for mine.

At approximately 3 A.M., the doctor on duty and a nurse gathered Beth and Rob, Lyn, Jane, and me into the private sitting room. He sat us down in the cramped space.

He told us that they had run extensive tests on Alison, and had done everything they could, but Alison was brain dead. Her heart was beating and the ventilator was helping her breathe, but still — she was brain dead. He said brain dead several times letting it sink in — brain dead...brain dead...brain dead. I guess he felt he had to make this as clear and as simple as possible.

Naturally we objected. She seemed unconscious, and now she is dead? What could be done? Would blood transfusions or any operation or procedure get results?

No. There was nothing that could be done. He described how children can sustain a whiplash so severe that it can either break the neck or dislodge the brain causing swelling and death. Also, Alison had stopped breathing for an extended period of time before she was resuscitated. He did not give a specific cause of death, but he indicated that these were the likely possibilities.

Then he explained that because Alison's heart had been restarted and she was being supported by a ventilator that the state of Maryland required the hospital to keep her on life support for twelve hours after this initial evaluation. If Alison's condition did not change, she would be declared legally dead. He stressed that this, however, was a formality as there was no indication of brain activity. Although her heart and lungs were working, they were not feeding a living body.

Beth grew quiet. Rob began to sob, "So there is nothing that can be done?"

"No, there is nothing that can be done.... There would have to be a complete reversal of this process.... Only a true miracle could save her.... By law she will continue on life support, but only as a formality." The doctor was sympathetic but stayed with the facts.

"There is another item I have to mention to you," the doctor started in. "Your daughter is an excellent candidate for organ donation. I know that this is a difficult subject, but we bring this up for those whose lives can be saved and helped by the life of Alison. No decision needs to be made now, but we ask you to consider this in the hours ahead. There is a window of time that we have to act in if you go forward with this after the twelve-hour period." This was difficult to hear, but it was said tactfully. No response was given.

Jane asked, "Did whiplash cause the red mark on her neck?"

"As I indicated," the doctor replied, "extremely quick movement of the neck can cause a subcutaneous or under-the-skin burn that shows through the skin as severe inflammation."

Beth left the room and returned to Alison. She had heard enough and knew where her place was. She quietly slipped out and took up her station that she would not leave for the next day and a half. Rob gradually grew more and more incoherent. He moaned and cried and began walking around the ward. He was inconsolable. A hospital guard came and led Rob and Lyn downstairs so Rob could see a psychiatrist. We heard in the morning that Rob had been taken to Sheppard Pratt Psychiatric Hospital and had been admitted for observation and for his own safety.

A WEEK AND A LIFETIME EARLIER — OCTOBER 9, 1995

The day was sunny and bright, that delightful early autumn weather on the East Coast. It was Columbus Day (well, Columbus Day celebrated anyway) and Beth's children had the day off from school. She asked if I would like to join them in the afternoon for lunch with Tom and Soraya Howard and their family. Jane and John Parker would be there with their three girls as well. Beth called when they were ready to eat, and I was able to come for a late lunch.

I had never been to Soraya's and I came around the back of the house where I heard voices. I saw all of the gathered children and got a big welcome hug from Alison. The children had their own lunch area on the downstairs porch. I went upstairs and Tom and Soraya were there with Jane, John, and Beth. I got a plate of food and joined the adults on the upstairs porch.

We ate, talked, and enjoyed the lovely day. The food was fresh and delicious and I was glad that I had taken the time off from work. The children were having dessert and Alison came upstairs to get some apple crisp. Jane's daughter, Kristen (Alison's shadow!) was following her and they were bounding around with high energy. Alison came running out of the house with a bowl of apple crisp and her foot slammed into the high door jamb dividing the house from the upstairs deck. She went sprawling — the dessert went flying.

Nothing was damaged, but Alison was crying in pain. Beth watched, wanting Alison to work this through herself, to find strength inside and to learn, the way we all must, to heal ourselves. Also, Alison had been running in the house and was supposed to be staying downstairs with the other children. I waited too. She continued to cry. Still, I did nothing. We all watched her, and she was not letting up — not screaming, but crying hard and in pain.

Tom got up, tentatively, not knowing Alison well but moved by her suffering. He went over to her, gently leaning down to see what he could do. I got up and came over to her and I leaned down, too. She put her arms out and I picked her up. She was still sobbing. I squeezed her and opened my heart to her. And she opened herself as well.

As had happened at other times, I had a strong connection with Alison, an experience that we were completely joined and that there was no distance between us. I let my love flow into her and I could feel it working and healing. The heavy and hurt emotions were being released and replaced by feelings of betterment or love, some higher quality beyond my mind's discernment. All I knew was that this connection was true and that I needed to allow it to serve its purpose.

Alison's sobbing subsided after twenty or thirty seconds, but I could still feel the hurt inside of her. Was this the emotional remains of what had happened or was she still in pain? I decided it was better to err on the side of taking care of her, so I gave her another big hug, this one not as long as the last, but again going to that place of connection and healing between us.

"Are you okay?" I asked.

"Yes," she said nodding, wiping away the tears.

Tom had already started to clean up the apple crisp and Alison immediately joined in the job without being asked, wanting to take care of her responsibility. She finished cleaning up and then rejoined the other children. We found out later that Alison had been getting the dessert for Kristen's little sister, Emma, who was downstairs, and that it was not for herself. This was no surprise as Alison found joy in serving others around her.

I recognized later that I was given an opportunity to understand Alison with both my heart and mind through this experience, and that this little crisis was a gift for me. It was a blessing in disguise. I was given an unforgettable and tangible awareness of Alison, which was as true as the loss that inevitably followed.

ground zero

OCTOBER *16, 1995*

In those deep hours of the night I started another round of phone calls contacting Faith, Kay, and Charity again. Kay would fly into Baltimore–Washington International Airport in the morning and I would pick her up. Then, Faith and Charity would arrive by train in the afternoon and I would pick them up as well.

It was difficult to convey Alison's true condition: her heart was beating, she was breathing, but there was no life. We held onto the hope that there could be a turnaround, but the reality of the situation was clear at the hospital. As the night wore on, Alison began to take on fluid and her body began to swell. Gradually those beautiful, full hazel eyes were squeezed shut. All of the IV fluids were important to keep her from dehydrating.

Beth and I discussed the issue of organ donation. We did not reach any conclusion. I felt that organ donation made sense, but I did not want to influence Beth in this decision. It seemed that we were moving toward having Alison be an organ donor.

I split my time between calling family and friends, and supporting Beth any way I could. I was also trying to track down Adelyn, Beth's close friend of many years. I called Addie's father at 4:30 A.M. He was kind enough to pass on another number to me. It seemed that between 4:30 and sunup I had spoken to every one of Adelyn's relatives. I did eventually find her though, and she said that she would come to Beth's home near Washington the next evening.

The black sky started melting at 6:30 A.M. Dark night was being overtaken by dark blue. The impenetrable blue rose up and up forever. It was a very delicious blue over the city of Baltimore that October 16. From our seventh story window, the sky turned to lighter blue with the few wisps of clouds glowing bright orange. It was another beautiful day, but as each day reveals anew, so each yesterday must fall away. Day and night stood silently together. Wakefulness and sleep, ignorance and understanding, life and death — these opposites were found nakedly entwined, as less than either and more than both together.

As it was getting light, wheels were set in motion for the day. I called the Perdue family, Beth's carpool for school, and several close friends. What can one think of an early morning call from an unexpected source? I also called Dr. Razi, Beth's pediatrician. She had questions and advice and would send natural herbal formulas for Beth and Alison. I finally reached Beth's friend, Camilla Lake. She would join us later in the morning.

At one point, Beth went to the ladies' room for a few minutes and I tended Alison by myself. A new nurse, Pam, had just come on duty. I felt that I wanted to step out of the normal bounds of patient care with her. I wanted to let her know how unique and special

Alison was. I said something to her but got little response. Then, even though I was pushing things, I continued to talk about Alison. She acknowledged what I had said, but continued her work without further conversation. Sensing that there was no easy way to communicate my feelings about this, I dropped the subject.

Later I learned from our other nurse, Peggy, that Pam had first come to the ward as a mother with her child. Like Alison, her child had not lived but had received wonderful care from the staff in the pediatric intensive care unit. Pam had been moved by the experience and the care that her child received and had decided to become a nurse to share the gift of her love with others. In hindsight, I decided to "enlighten" the one person in the ward who appreciated the specialness of each child in her care, including Alison, in a way that I may never know.

After more calls to Beth's family, I spoke with Beth about Matthew and David. Beth decided that I should drive up to Lyn's to pick them up, and that they should be informed of the situation after they arrived at the hospital. As I was leaving, Beth said that if they asked for the truth — or if they asked whether Alison had died — that I should tell them. As I drove up that glorious morn, with most of the traffic going in the opposite direction, I felt that my life was also going against the grain. I got up to Lyn's house, and Laurie was with the children who had just awakened. Lyn was with Rob at Sheppard Pratt Hospital.

The boys were excited about the baseball game from the night before. Eli asked about Alison. "No change," I said not wanting to discuss details. We had a breakfast of cold cereal, which tasted strange after a night of no sleep. I was upbeat and wacky with the kids, I did not want them to have too much time to think. I went upstairs to call Beth's neighbor and Alison's soccer coach, Karil. The team practiced Monday afternoons. Karil and Beth were also close friends. I caught her as she was getting her children off to school, but I felt that this was my only chance. She had known

Alison for five years, and her daughter and Alison were good friends. She let out a cry of pain at the news, but I had no gentle way to break it to her.

The boys and I left for the hospital and we drove downtown in the long line of rush hour traffic. They were excited about the day off and having more time with Eli and Emily. We talked sports and traffic as we drove.

We spoke briefly about the accident. "There but for the grace of God go I," went through my mind as I drove the boys to the hospital.

"Is Daddy at the hospital?"

"He is at another hospital with Lyn. He is very upset about Alison being hurt in the accident."

As we got closer to the hospital, Matthew and David started to ask more questions about Alison. By the time we got to the parking garage the whole story was coming out.

"Boys," I said, "this is the most important day of your lives. When Alison had her accident last night she was hurt badly. The doctors have worked very hard on her to get her through this, but they have not been able to help her. She's…" at this point I did not know what word to use and I hesitated, searching.

"…gone to heaven," Matthew said.

"Yes," I said, "that's right Matthew. Alison has gone to heaven, and we should pray for her. She is with God now."

We got out of the car, and I put my arms around them as we walked. I did not know how this was going to be for them. Inside the hospital we had to sign in. When the person at the desk found out who the boys were, she was especially swift and helpful. We went upstairs to the pediatric ward and I took the boys into the private sitting room. It was becoming our home base and was quite comfortable.

Our nurse, Pam, joined us to help answer any questions. She brought a Polaroid picture that she had just taken of Alison to show to the boys in case seeing her changed physical condition was frightening or difficult for them. Beth came in from Alison's bedside to be with the boys and to explain everything to them.

I started in. "I told the boys on the way up here that Alison's accident was worse than we thought. I told them that Alison is in heaven now."

Matthew nodded.

"Yes," Beth began matter-of-factly, "Alison has died and —"

Matthew looked startled. Obviously "gone to heaven," and "died," meant very different things to him. He was upset and started to cry. David remained quiet at first, but eventually he started to cry, too. Beth encouraged both boys to express their feelings, especially David because of his initial reluctance to do so. Pam showed the boys the picture of Alison with the IV tubes coming out of her, the neck brace, and the beautiful quilt. The boys had no trouble with her appearance and went directly in to be with their sister. Beth asked Matthew and David to pray for Alison, and she had the boys touch her and connect with her body. The boys stayed for some time with Beth and Alison while I stayed in the waiting room, so that Beth could have this private time with her three children.

Johns Hopkins staff helps to bring families closer together in loss. A little ritual employed in the pediatric ward is to have children make prints of their deceased sibling's hands in a rubber-like mold. This dries and plaster is poured into the mold, which then sets up. Beth and I each took one of the boys and helped them put Alison's hands into the mold trays for a good imprint. This was a small but touching exercise in sharing loss and recognizing finality. Beth keeps these plaster molds in a cubby in her home devoted to Alison. They are heart shaped with her handprints in the middle.

Afterward, I had to leave for the airport to pick up Kay. Beth decided that I should take the boys with me. I would return with Kay and then drop the boys at Lyn's house where they could spend the rest of the day with their cousins.

MAKING ARRANGEMENTS

Camilla arrived bearing a box of medicinal herbs that are used for strengthening the body in a time of crisis. She joined Beth and Jane at Alison's bedside. Soon a group of doctors needed to see

Alison alone. Beth and her friends were asked to wait in the sitting room. Here, Beth asked Camilla to call the woman she worked for, Leslie, and apprise her of the situation. Alone with her two friends in the sitting room, Beth's thoughts turned to the unavoidable.

"I think it's time to begin to look at funeral arrangements," she said. "Will you both help me in what I need to do?"

Beth asked who they would recommend as a minister. Camilla spoke highly of Rev. Richard Dancey, a priest of the Christian Community Church.

"If I was in your place, Beth," she said, "I would ask him to perform the funeral service."

The Christian Community Church was founded in the early twentieth century. Protestant ministers sought guidance from Rudolf Steiner, the Austrian social philosopher, in renewing Christian rituals of celebrating the sacraments. The blessing is, "The Father God be in us. The Son God create in us. The Spirit God enlighten us."

Beth had been introduced to Steiner's ideas through the Waldorf school system. Her children attended the Washington Waldorf School and she found Steiner's holistic approach to education inspirational and insightful. Beth had occasionally attended Rev. Dancey's once-a-month services when he came down from Pennsylvania. These were held at a Waldorf preschool center near her home in Silver Spring, Maryland, just north of Washington, D.C.

In the church service, the blessing "Christ in You" is often repeated. The services were different than those of her Episcopalian upbringing, yet they were enlivening and spiritual. Beth knew no other ministers and was comfortable with Rev. Dancey. "Would he come?" was the next question. Rev. Dancey was called and agreed to lead the service.

MONDAY MORNING CARPOOL

"You haven't heard?!" a friend asked Lark Bergwin-Anderson as she dropped off her children at school. Lark knew Beth and her children well. She was shocked and dumbfounded when she learned the news.

"Go get Sheila," a voice in Lark's mind spoke. "Have her get her lyre and go to the hospital to be with Alison and Beth. Have her find out what Beth needs and do it!"

Lark turned to her friend.

"I must get Sheila," she said, "and have her bring her lyre to Baltimore to be with Beth and Alison. She is needed at the hospital."

It was clear to Lark that she was acting as an instrument, responding to a call from deep within.

Five minutes later, Lark arrived at Sheila Johns' house. Sheila was in tears. She had already heard the news. Sheila, a lyre player, had attended seminars on the role of music in harmonizing life changes.

The women embraced. Lark told Sheila that she should go to the hospital and help Alison and Beth. Sheila was uncertain about this undertaking — she did not know where to go in Baltimore and she was also concerned about barging in on Beth and her family at the hospital. She wanted to help, but she was hesitant.

Lark fixed Sheila in her gaze.

"Sheila," she said quietly, "what have you been training for?"

Sheila immediately called Sandi Chamberlin, a close mutual friend, and asked her if she would drive her to Baltimore. Sandi was happy to do so and the two women quickly got a few things together. They had heard that Alison would be pulled off life support, and Sheila wanted to have time to play the lyre. They also made arrangements for their children to be picked up at school if they ran a little late. Their idea was for Sheila to play for half an hour before the life support was removed and then they would return home. They could always stay a little longer if need be.

Sandi would prove to be invaluable in the days ahead. She had said that she would help with anything, and I found she always had an effortless solution for the many dilemmas I brought her.

Lark stayed at home and worked on other preparations for the upcoming days. She also had a large natural-wood-framed painting of Raphael's *Madonna and Child* that, along with soothing lavender oil, she gave to Sandi to bring to the hospital.

An hour later, Sheila and Sandi arrived at Johns Hopkins Hospital armed with a lyre and selfless commitment. In they strode to the pediatric intensive care unit: the *Madonna and Child*, the lyre, Sheila, and Sandi. They greeted Beth and Alison lovingly and began to settle in. The painting was placed in a window overlooking the mother and child below.

Then Sheila asked Beth if she would like her to play the lyre. Beth nodded. Sheila started playing softly and gently, the graceful and beautiful sounds of the lyre massaging the environment, smoothing the rough edges of the hospital, settling and soothing, transcending the ringing bells and whistles around Alison and Beth. It was the perfect backdrop of harmony in this room with four children in critical care, three fighting for their lives and one having gone to heaven.

REMEMBERING THE QUARRY

Alison was five "but nearly six" the first time we went to the quarry together. It was a summer day in Vermont, warm in the sun, cool in the shade. The quarry was on a main road and was frequented by a variety of people. The marble was a beautiful grayish-white, and the turquoise water shone in the bright sunlight. This, the first quarry of several, was about a football field in length and fifty feet wide. It was impossible to tell how deep it was, but it seemed a long way to the bottom.

As we climbed a well-used footpath, we reached an area where people congregated and sunned themselves. There were some crude ladders that went up a level to the quarries beyond. There was also a side pool here jutting out from the main pool. Most of those gathered were young people. Those who made use of this area respected the gift of the land and water, and enjoyed it immensely.

Swimmers would climb up the two small ladders to a footpath. There were several jumping spots along the path, the first at the corner of the side pool and the main pool with water on three sides. From a height of seventeen feet they could dive, or fly, or twirl, or flip, or flop into the water below. There were screams and hoots and laughter and splashing — and silence as individuals took their turns off the rock corner and higher places beyond.

I went up and took the plunge by jumping off. It was a good height and the water was cool and invigorating. I jumped off several times while Beth stayed with the children swimming in the main pool. Then I joined them in the water. The children wanted to go up to the jumping point where I had been, so Beth and I climbed the ladders with them. When we got there, they all peered over the edge — and it looked a long way down.

Alison said, "I want to go off," but then she looked over the edge and decided it was too high.

"I don't know — but I want to do it."

"What do you think, Pat?" Beth said.

"It isn't that far," I said, "but…"

We talked about it and the boys also expressed an interest. Finally, we decided that since Alison was more of a dog-paddler than a swimmer, and because we did not want her plunging to the bottom of the great abyss, that she should wear her life vest, "If you really want to do this!"

The older boys were hesitant, but Alison was intent. (You could tell that she was nervous by the running dialogue she kept up with herself, asking questions and making statements, but always moving closer to the brink.) It was decided. She was going to do it. I jumped in ahead of her and came out on the other side of the pool area in case she needed help. I watched, wondering whether she was really going to do it. She got up her courage, stood on the lip of the quarry, and jumped. She hit the water and in a split second bobbed up. I burst into applause as did other onlookers from the rocks.

"Way to go, Alison!" I shouted. She was blowing water out of her nose and began her "crawl" to the take-out point. She was happy. She had overcome her fear and done it!

"That a girl, Alison!"

She was the only one of the children to make the jump that year.

FORMULAS AND REMEDIES

Stephie Carmody gave Lark a call to find out if anyone could take some essential oils and health remedies to Beth. Sheila and Sandi had already left. Since Stephie, a nurse, had a continuing education class near Baltimore, she decided to make a quick stop at the hospital and drop off the items for Beth. Stephie had recently attended a seminar with Lark on death and dying, and she wanted to encourage Beth. She put the items into her backpack, which serves as her home away from home, a repository of healing formulas, herbal remedies, and helpful medications, and somehow found her way to the hospital in the midst of Baltimore.

ARRIVALS

The boys and I went to the airport to pick up their Aunt Kay. However, I had not bothered to ask for directions and ended up taking a roundabout route. It was a long trip and we arrived about forty minutes late. Kay was getting ready to take a cab by the time we got there. I apologized and walked over to the closest rental car location to get a map.

The trip back was quick and direct. Kay talked with the boys about what had happened. The boys loved being with Kay, and I was happy that Beth's family was starting to arrive. When we returned to Johns Hopkins to drop her off, I got out of the car to talk with her about Alison's condition. I had not wanted to share all of the details in front of the boys. Kay felt that there might still be hope. I knew it sounded conflicting because Alison was breathing and her heart was still beating, but, in reality, she was gone from us. I spoke plainly to Kay, relating the doctor's findings and telling her about Alison's physical changes.

Kay went to the lobby and signed in as I headed back to Lyn's house with the boys. She went upstairs and found Beth at Alison's side.

Beth had been doing well. She was with Alison, caring for her every need, available for whatever needed attention — following this process to its inevitable conclusion. She was standing and waiting, serving her dear departed daughter.

Aunt Kay, Alison's loving aunt, entered. She came in and in her eyes was the knowledge, the realization, that all hope was gone. Beth's eyes met Kay's and in that moment all that was held back in Beth, willing herself to be strong for Alison, erupted. A wave of pent-up emotions poured forth, the two sisters held each other and cried. Nurse Pam heard the cries of anguish and rushed in. She was told that Beth's sister had arrived, the first family member, someone to help shoulder this burden and someone upon whose shoulders this burden would fall heavily.

I drove the boys back to Lyn's, managed to get lost again, and then with the boys' help found the house. I returned to Johns Hopkins and waited to pick up Faith and Charity. Again, I was greeted warmly as I entered the hospital.

I was told that John Knox, Beth's dad, was coming with Sue, his wife. They lived near Syracuse, New York, about four hundred miles from Baltimore, but as they would tell everyone, "It's only seven hours away." They eventually made it down by 3 P.M.

At Johns Hopkins, a small group of women had now gathered, giving Beth support and making arrangements for Alison's body. The lyre music soothed and softened the room. Alison's curtain was partially drawn for privacy.

Stephie had arrived around lunchtime. Because she knew Beth only as an acquaintance from school, she did not want to impose or intrude on her. This hesitancy on the part of those who care and genuinely want to help is common, but those in crisis need us. All of us have something to give and it is our willingness to help that makes a difference, more so than any skills and aptitudes we bring. Yes, Beth needed help. As much as everyone wanted to protect her privacy, Beth needed the support, love, and knowledge of those around her to guide her through the many decisions in front of her. She had never been through anything remotely like this, and the many changes and the emotional shock crashed down on her in a torrent.

Beth needed support in many ways, some of which she did not even know. She had a clear idea of what her desires were, but she did not know how to put them into practice, nor what was possible, practical, or legal. Beth had decided to care for Alison at home. Stephie tentatively stepped in. She spoke with the funeral director about Beth's desire to bring Alison back home from the hospital and not have her embalmed. He termed her request, "highly unusual," but began to make plans to fulfill these requests. Stephie counseled Beth that if her desire was to keep close to Alison that she should absolutely act on that and not give up that control to anyone. She also told Beth that an around-the-clock vigil could be held in Alison's honor; there could be someone in constant attendance with Alison over the next days while she was at home before the funeral. Lark was already arranging a schedule for everyone interested in participating in the vigil. Stephie then approached the hospital staff and let the doctor know that there was a religious objection to performing an autopsy. The doctor indicated that an autopsy did not seem necessary.

Stephie spent a lot of time with Beth and Alison, and often found herself talking to Alison: "How are you doing?" "I am sending my love to you." "What can I do to help this situation?" "Is there anything I can do for you?"

This is something many of us do when we are around a loved one who has passed on. It is a way of coming to grips with the loss and sending our love and good intentions to them. And yet, it is more like a dialogue than an emotion-laden monologue. There is often a feeling that they are all right and that their time had come to leave here. Sometimes there is an experience of more than this, of a true conversation with specific questions, answers, and requests.

After spending time with Alison, Stephie felt assured and comforted. "Many of us have a connection with a loved one who has died, yet we think of it as a reaction to the death or a vivid imagination. The truth is that many of us get reassurance, guidance, and a true sense of peace from what is often a real communication with a loved one. We just don't recognize it as such."

I left to pick up Faith and Charity at the train station. There was plenty of time, but even with the map, I overshot the area, got cut off by one-way streets, and became totally confused. Somehow, I finally came upon it. Inside I found Faith and Charity sitting on their suitcases. I apologized for my lateness and we made our way back to the hospital. Again, it was not clear to them that Alison had died. I was trying to be gentle, but I let them know what had transpired. Back at Johns Hopkins, the people at the desk seemed to know us on sight and upstairs the lyre music played on.

1,000 MOMMIES

One night, like many others, as Beth put the children to bed, they said their prayers together:

> From head to foot
> I am made in the image of God.
>
> From my heart right into my hands
> I feel the breath of God.
>
> When I speak with my mouth
> I follow the will of God.
>
> When I behold God everywhere,
> in father, in mother, in all dear people, in
> animals and flowers, in trees and stones,
>
> Nothing can fill me with fear, but only with love
> for all that is about me.

> I look up into the hills whence cometh my help,
>
> My help cometh from the Lord
> who made heaven and earth.
>
> He will not suffer my foot to slip.
>
> He that keepeth me will not slumber nor sleep.
>
> The Lord is my keeper and my shade.
>
> He is beside me at my right hand.

Beth and Alison frolicking on May Day, 1994.

After kissing the boys good night, Beth was tucking Alison in. The story had been read, the day had been talked about, and Alison was thinking, lying comfortably in her bed.

"Mommy," she said gazing up, "if I had a thousand mommies to choose from, I would pick you to be my mommy." There was a thoughtful pause. "Even if some of them were nicer than you," she now directed a smile at Beth, her eyes twinkling, "I would still pick you!"

SEMPER FIDELIS

When Rob was taken to Sheppard Pratt Hospital, he was very much alone. His wife, Lyn, and brother, John, were supporting him, but he was confined to a room with an attendant at all times so that he would not hurt himself. He said that he just wanted to die — and he meant it. He was alone in his heart and virtually alone in his struggle. That first day, as the angels of mercy descended to comfort, hold, and heal the deep wounds at Johns Hopkins, Rob was isolated and in despair.

Richard and Janice Burris had known Beth and Rob for years. When they heard about the accident, they dropped everything and headed over to the hospital. Richard dropped his wife off at Johns Hopkins Hospital. He took on the mission of getting through to Rob and proceeded on to Sheppard Pratt. He did not know what he was going to do, but he felt that there was a man alone and in pain, and his help was needed.

Like myself, Richard had taken a men's seminar and it had changed his life. Well, actually, it doesn't change the lives of men, it allows men to be who they are — and enjoy it! Men realize that at a truly intimate level they are the same, "We're all just a bunch of — jerks!" There is liberation in that and an acceptance. There is a welcoming of power that comes with men being men, in their guts not in their heads, an esprit de corps.

Richard had a mission. A man he knew and had known for years was in trouble, serious trouble, and Richard was not going to sit idly by. He had two daughters himself and, as he told me later,

"If I had been driving a car in which one of my girls had been killed, I'd be suicidal too."

Yes, someone had to think of Rob, alone and without the support to bring him through, so Richard drove to Sheppard Pratt. He did not have a plan, but he did have a mission — as a retired marine fighter pilot in Vietnam, as a man in the men's movement, he was ready to wing it.

Unbeknownst to him, Lyn was there supporting Rob, doing whatever could be done, and John, Rob's brother, was also with him. It was an incredibly difficult time for both of them, and in a sense, there was not much support: Rob's father was in a retirement home and had become very reclusive since his wife's death two years before. Rob's other sibling, Wayne, the eldest, was a violent man with a psychopathic history. He was serving a long prison sentence in the Maryland penitentiary system. Rob had all of the help that he could count on from his immediate family. As far as the rest, the many relatives, Rob was in no condition to see them, nor did he want to see anyone.

Then the Marines showed up. Richard arrived at the ward where Rob was staying.

"I'd like to see Rob Sanders," he told the guard at the desk.

"No one but the immediate family is allowed to see Mr. Sanders at present."

"Yes, of course. I understand," Richard said stalling for time, thinking, thinking... *"Into the valley of Death, Rode the six hundred..."* "I'm Rob Sanders' brother and I've come to see him," he said.

"I will let them know you are here. You will need to sign in."

"Yes, thank you. Oh, unfortunately in my rush to get over here, I left my wallet at home."

The guard found someone to cover the front desk for him and went to Rob's room.

"Excuse me," he said addressing Lyn, "there is a visitor here for Mr. Sanders. It's his brother and he doesn't have any ID. I'm going to have to have you verify him for me."

Lyn and John looked at each other in amazement. Now what?!! They were dumbfounded. The images conjured up were too bizarre to consider. Because Rob's brother was incarcerated, there was no way he could be there. Was this a joke? Had Wayne really come? Had he escaped prison to visit Rob in this psychiatric hospital?

Needless to say, and for reasons too numerous to mention, Richard never got in to see Rob — and he never gave up on him either. I do know a few people who, in the next days, went to Sheppard Pratt to meditate and pray for Rob in their cars. But no one else went directly to be with Rob, to share his pain, to be "his brother," and to let him know that he was not alone. In a significant and mysterious way, we walk this life together. What Richard Burris did should not be overlooked.

Nights with the Children

There was many a night when one (or all) of the children wanted to sleep with Beth in her bed. I often had the task of taking the child who had gone to sleep in Beth's room upstairs to bed. Matthew was so big that he would be "sleepwalked" upstairs, but David and Alison needed to be carried. Alison, being the youngest, naturally enjoyed sleeping in Mommy's bed more than the boys. Often, I would carry her upstairs at night before Beth and I went to bed.

There was one night when I wanted to watch TV downstairs, so shortly after she lay down I checked to see if she was asleep. My timing seemed good, so I gently pulled her up in my arms and began to carry her upstairs.

As we were quietly going upstairs, she cocked open her eyes and said, "I'm still awake. But it's okay." Then she resumed her sleeping attitude, a conspirator in the charade. She obviously enjoyed the "being carried" part as much as the "sleeping in Mommy's bed" part.

Gathering Support

As I waited near the elevator that goes directly to the pediatric ward, a building service man saw me. He eyed me for a second and then asked how it was going with the little girl upstairs. I shared the situation with him briefly; it seemed that the whole hospital moved to support us in our need, and employees who knew of Alison were silently rooting for us. Friends and family were gradually gathering, the nurses treated us with care, and the staff and the doctors went out of their way to accommodate us. There was rising love and support in dealing with this tragedy, and everywhere I went, there was a helping hand and an encouraging word.

Stephie was at the hospital all afternoon, and there came a point when she felt that she should leave and give Beth's family time alone with Alison. Although she felt useful, she did not want to be in the way or a hindrance. She was torn about leaving but finally decided to go. She quietly went out to the lobby elevators and pushed the "down" button. She waited as the two elevators slowly ascended. She waited as they slowly did their loading and unloading. Both elevators passed her floor and continued their slow climb. She waited and waited. Time passed. The elevators were not coming for her.

She had second thoughts about leaving. "Maybe there's a reason I'm here," she thought to herself, "and maybe there's a reason that I should stay."

She turned and went back to Beth and Alison — her place was there. Her knowledge and help, medical background, and thoughtful awareness were all needed. She stayed and gave Sheila a back rub in between hours of playing the lyre. She made arrangements with the funeral director for Alison to be picked up the next day, and she conferred with the hospital staff on medical matters until late in the evening.

Late in the afternoon, Jack Petrash, Matthew's teacher of five years, arrived. I was pleased to see Jack; his caring, conscious manner and his optimism were a breath of fresh air. Also, there had only been women with Beth and it was nice to have another guy around. There was a large family of friends and loved ones gathered around Alison now. We had created our own environment of music, light, and accouterments in the sterile hospital setting. The Johns

Hopkins staff was helpful and did everything possible to make our experience meaningful.

Beth's greatest desire was to stay with Alison and to continue to care for her during this time. This meant that Beth wanted to bring Alison back home and have her among her family and friends. Lark had done research on funeral homes in the Washington, D.C. area and found only one that would accommodate Beth's desire to bring Alison home. Negotiations went on. Because Alison had died in the hospital, hospital regulations stipulated that she could only be released to a funeral home. The negotiations were concluded and the funeral home agreed to pick up Alison when she was released by the hospital.

REMEMBERING ALISON'S SICK DAY

On a very important day for Beth, the day before the Fall Bazaar at the Waldorf School, Alison got sick. This was terrible timing. Beth had planned for months to help ready the school for the big fund-raiser, and she asked if I could help out since I worked from my home. It was a busy workday, but we arranged that Alison would come over in the afternoon to be with me.

I worked on the phone in sales and marketing, so I asked Alison if she wanted to rest in the room next to mine. Instead she wanted to stay with me. After a short time, she fell asleep, and for the next several hours I did my work as quietly as possible. I would look over at her periodically, a little sleeping angel in my room. My work did not disturb her, and eventually she awoke feeling much better. Although I may not have accomplished as much as possible on that day, having Alison with me made it far more enjoyable.

Alison was also quite practical. The Sanders' family life had been turned upside down for some years previous to the time that Beth and I were together. Once, a short while after I had been with Beth, Alison came up to me and said, "Pat, I like it when you are here. My mom is much happier when you're around." I understood that this was more a comment on her experience than a compliment for me. Alison was sharing an improvement in her home life and appreciating the fact that I was a part of that.

FINAL PRONOUNCEMENT

Late in the afternoon, John Parker, Jane's husband, brought Kristen, their daughter, to the hospital to be with Alison. Alison and Kristen were great friends. The adults felt that Kristen should have the opportunity to see Alison and to experience the care and love that surrounded her.

Beth was braiding her daughter's hair when Kristen entered. She had already taken a lock of Alison's hair as a keepsake. Jane asked if Kristen could have a lock of hair as well and Beth cut another lock as a remembrance for her. Kristen participated in events at the hospital, and later I saw her leading children to see Alison at Beth's house, guiding them into this new territory with complete familiarity and ease. Alison was still Kristen's friend; it was just that her friend was no longer there.

It was getting near the witching hour, when the final pronouncement would be made regarding Alison, but as the doctor had said the night before, this would only be a formality. Dr. Kyle was on duty that Monday and had the job of determining Alison's condition after the twelve-hour time period.

Beth wanted to be in constant attendance to Alison, she wanted to take Alison home, and she also wanted to have Alison's body disturbed as little as possible. For these reasons and other deeply held beliefs, Beth decided not to have Alison be an organ donor. I am sure that the hospital was disappointed. Alison was strong and supple in mind and body. She was, in fact, an "excellent candidate." There was still a vital role, however, that Alison's body would play in the days ahead.

Beth discovered in her discussions with Rev. Dancey and others that there were many aspects of caring for the body and funeral arrangements that were within her control. There is general ignorance about after-death care, and few people create an outcome of their choosing. Beth exercised choices that kept her close to Alison in these difficult days, and she opted against invasive procedures such as embalming.

Those assembled gathered at Alison's bedside as Dr. Kyle made the rounds at 4 P.M. and stated what appeared to be obvious: there was no neurological functioning and Alison was dead. Beth asked for some time to be with Alison. About 6 P.M., we all gathered to have the life support removed and our new nurse, Philamina, had already started that process. Beth asked if this could be delayed. The funeral home was unable to come so late in the day and Beth did not want the life support removed. Dr. Kyle was summoned.

I had had some time to get familiar with the doctor and had looked Kyle over: short hair, functional glasses, pants worn high, slight build, competent. Kyle seemed a nice enough guy. We all gathered, Beth, Faith, John and Sue Knox, Kay, Charity, Jane, Camilla, Sandi, Sheila, Stephie, Jack, and four or five other close friends.

I presented our case to the doctor. It was too late for the funeral home to pick up Alison that day, and Beth did not want Alison spending the night in the morgue alone; Beth felt it important that a loved one be with Alison during this time. It would also be Beth's last night with her daughter. The question was put to Dr. Kyle: can Alison be kept on life support tonight and then taken off early in the morning before the funeral home comes to bring her back to Beth's house?

Dr. Kyle responded, "If you were waiting on your father from out of town and he couldn't make it until 7 A.M., and you wanted him to see Alison as she is now, still breathing, I would say yes, so I don't see why I can't do this for you as well."

We were thrilled that the doctor had been able to see things our way and support Beth in her desires, even this unusual one. To express this, I turned and slapped the doctor on the shoulder and said, "What a man!"

We were all thankful and expressed it. The doctor went off to continue the rounds and we began to make plans. John Knox, Sue, and Faith would go to Beth's house in Silver Spring, Maryland. Jane would go home with Camilla and leave us her car for transporting the boys and new arrivals back to Beth's the next day. Charity and Kay would stay the night at the hospital with Beth and me. Sandi and Sheila would go home and return in the morning for the removal of life support.

Finally, Jane turned to me and said, "What a man?!! That —" she said with emphasis, "was a woman!!"

To tell you the truth, I hadn't been sure. I was taken aback by Jane's attack. I had tried my best to tell. Kyle certainly was hiding the fact pretty well!

"I wasn't sure. However," I said further prejudicing my case, "I thought it best to give her the benefit of the doubt."

"She probably liked it," Jane conceded. "All of the women here knew," she said condescendingly. She seemed genuinely happy to have such a clear-cut case of male idiocy into which she could sink her teeth.

"Hey, what do I know? I'm just a guy, a jerk. Why would any woman choose to be like me!"

SKI ADVENTURE

It was our first day of skiing and the sky was overcast. Beth tried to take the children skiing every year. Having grown up in New England, she wished to share this with them. As a single parent this was a difficult undertaking, especially when the children were young. She would be out on the bunny slope with Alison between her legs, holding Matthew's hand, and shouting instructions to little David as they made their way down the slope. The children could all ski reasonably well now and Alison, at 6, was as good as either of the boys.

We had had a full day on the slopes. Darkness was coming on, but there was time for one more run. Earlier that day I had gone on a trail by myself that looked a little difficult for the children, and I decided to do it again. The top part was steep with only a thin trail of skiable snow. Then the trail widened, following an up-and-down course that eventually connected to the main run down the mountain. It was fun and exciting and not too difficult once you got past the first part. I told Beth I wanted to go and Alison said she would like to join me. I told the boys what trail we were going on and they thought it too challenging and had no interest. Alison was up for it.

We went up the chair lift talking chitter-chatter pitter-patter about this and that. I had my arm around her and was enjoying the immense beauty of the mountain area. When we got to the top, we came off and went to the steep beginning that funneled into the trail below. It was not a long distance to where the trail flattened out, but the top was too steep and thin to effectively make turns on. When we stopped, I told Alison I would go ahead, and I asked her to wait until I called from below. I went down the steep section and around a turn and came to a stop. I made my way back up the trail, but I still could not see her. I yelled to her that it would be all right for her to keep coming.

A few seconds later, this little daring ball of skier appeared as if out of nothing, flying downhill crouched with hands clutching her ski poles. I have a picture in my mind of this determined little girl, on the edge, yet in control.

Let go and let God.

NIGHTFALL

Things settled down after Dr. Kyle's visit. It had been a long day for everyone. A calm descended — the calm after the storm and the flurry of activity. There were hugs, kisses, and a few more tears as those who were going home prepared to do so. John Knox and Sue drove with Faith Knox to Beth's house for the night. Beth inadvertently gave them the wrong exit number from the Washington Beltway, and there was a little misadventure with Mr. Knox, Mrs. Knox, and Ms. Knox in the car. When they got to Beth's home, they cleaned the house from top to bottom preparing it for Alison's return and the many family and friends to follow.

spirit in the night

Jane was leaving with Camilla, and I went outside with them to get Jane's car so we could have it for the next day. We went through one of the side lobbies downstairs, and the guard gave a warm "Hello" as we entered the parking garage. We got into Camilla's car and drove outside. It was dark and Jane was not sure where she had parked her car. We drove around a street or two, then we came to an intersection.

"This is it," Jane said cautiously. "This is where I parked my car." There were no vehicles where she pointed.

"It's gone," she said flatly. We continued slowly forward into the next block.

Suddenly Jane lit up. "There it is!" she shouted.

The car was at the next corner, parked next to a fire hydrant. It had been sitting illegally parked for the entire day. We thought that the security guards must have known the car and not ticketed or towed it on purpose.

I got in to move it and decided that I would go for food. I drove around and found myself cruising the drab inner city. Again, I felt isolated and without clear direction. All of this getting lost was draining and disconcerting. We were all trying to find a new way in an often inhospitable land. I gave up after a short while and headed back to the hospital, a place of refuge if not hope.

At the front desk I was again welcomed warmly. Our nurse, Peggy, must have put out the word to security after my talk with her about my difficulties from the night before. Things had been in a flux then, but Alison had been alive, and we still had hope. Now it was finished — in truth before it had begun. We were embraced by change and could not escape. We had say over the wheres and whens of our circumstances, but not over what would happen.

Around the corner, a small cafeteria that served sandwiches was open all night. I brought some food upstairs. Before I ate I went in to see Beth. To my surprise, she was in the bed with Alison.

Beth had wanted to be with Alison and share this time with her. She had wanted to get in bed with her but was unsure about it. Stephie had encouraged her to do so; many parents spend the night with their children in the hospital. Stephie's short visit had lengthened and lengthened and ended only when she tucked Beth in after a long day of intensively caring for her and Alison. When I came over to Beth, she had a troubled look on her face. She looked at me, torn between a mother's desire to be with her daughter, whom she loves beyond measure, and lying in bed with this dead body beside her.

"Is this all right?" she said with her eyes, and whole body. "Am I doing something wrong? Is this something so self-indulgent that it goes beyond the already weird boundaries of this situation?" I understood the delicate nature of her feelings. I felt a tug, actually a hard pull, at the fabric of life that had already been torn.

We embrace this life through our bodies, but the body is a container for the spirit. Beth was experiencing the essence of this. Shouldn't she reject the body and go inside to the true spirit? Yet, Alison's body *was* Beth's body, and more to the point, Alison's spirit was Beth's spirit. She was Beth, she had come from Beth, she had come through Beth, she had lived on Beth's life energy. How could Beth reject who she herself was? Alison's body and spirit were interwoven with Beth's own, yet they were also separate and unique. Now Alison's spirit was gone from her body. For Beth, the loss of Alison's spirit was an earthquake whose aftershocks and tremors would go on and on in the months and years to come. That spirit was now heaven-sent. The loss of the physical form in which that relationship had taken place was the next inevitable step. It would only be a short time before Alison's body would go through its own transformation, opposite to that of the spirit, and return to the earth.

"Beth, it's fine," I said giving her a kiss.

"Is it really, Pat?" she said.

"Yes," I said. "This will be the last night you will be able to spend with Alison. I think that it will help you to be closer to her."

She settled back with Alison, feeling more at home now, the two of them snug in a hospital bed. I went back to the sitting room to get something to eat. Beth was with Alison's breathing, lifeless body in the care of the angels of mercy, knowing full well the dichotomy of this moment, but choosing to live in unity instead.

That evening, Charity spoke with Rev. Dancey by phone. They discussed whether to have the funeral service on Thursday or Friday. Charity indicated that some family members might have to leave Friday and Rev. Dancey agreed to have the service on Thursday, October 19. The funeral would be held at 1 P.M. The next question was whether Rev. Dancey could come to visit Beth at the hospital. Yes, he would come that night, sometime.

The sitting room was lit only by a lamp when I came in. It was comfortable and the soft light gave it a warm feeling. I shared the food I brought with Kay and Charity. Afterwards, I went back to Beth and Alison.

I looked at what had gathered in the room with Alison — there was the *Madonna and Child* in the window, the lyre and lyre player at the foot of the bed, the quilted bedspread, a rosary, homeopathic remedies, herbal formulas, prayer beads, holy water from India, prayer books, and other gifts of spirit. Nearly everyone who came brought something that they thought might make a small difference for Beth; all who came brought hearts full of compassion and love.

Sheila was playing the lyre again. It was actually not "again" but continuing on and on in time, into night, into dawn, into darkness, into light, into death, into parting, into eternity. She played and played for hours on end, and yes here she was, playing again. I came over to the side of the bed and pulled up a chair. I was next to Beth with Alison beside her, two peas in a pod. They were waiting for Rev. Dancey.

Sandi wanted to read a spiritual work for Beth and Alison. She decided to read from the Bible. She chose St. John's Gospel and started in. I was sitting in a chair with my head next to Beth. The lyre was going and the words flowed forth, the story of Christ's life: "In the beginning was the Word and the Word was with God, and the Word was God. The same was in the beginning with God. All things were made by him; and without him was not any thing made that was made. In him was life; and the life was the light of men. And the light shineth in darkness; and the darkness comprehended it not..." and Beth was resting with Alison, listening, being, drifting here and there, being with her daughter, drifting, listening, being.

Then my head came up, my arm was asleep. St. John was still speaking the words of the life of Christ and the sounds of the celestial hosts were still reverberating through the strings of the lyre. My body had been asleep too.

"Then the same day at evening being the first day of the week, when the doors were shut where the disciples were assembled because of fear, came Jesus and stood in the midst, and saith unto them, 'Peace be unto you....'"

I got up and stumbled back into the side room with Charity and Kay. One was on the couch and the other on the floor. Fortunately, there was enough room for me to lie down as well and get a few hours sleep.

REVEREND DANCEY

At 1 A.M., when Sandi and Sheila finished reading St. John's Gospel and playing the lyre, they went to the entrance lounge of the pediatric ward. They stretched out on the cold chairs under the fluorescent lights to get some rest. They decided to stay the night rather than go home for a few hours only to return early in the morning when the life support would be taken off of Alison. Their "half-hour visit" had stretched and stretched, becoming timeless in its witness to the events at hand.

Beth dozed after nearly two days of non-stop life-changing intensity. She was with Alison in a dreamworld far from the cold reality she had come to know. All was quiet except for the machines and their needs and Philamina checking in occasionally. Beth slept in the quiet of the night, the quiet of the night and the bliss of sleep, and the bliss of ignorance, the ignorance in bliss, the ignorance of the pain, the ignorance of the loss, yes, the bliss…the blisss…the blissss…

She stirred and looked up. The quiet, the quiet night, the quiet man in the quiet night. Rev. Dancey had come. It was after 2 A.M. and he had made the hour-and-a-half drive down from Pennsylvania to be with her and Alison. He was taking it in. The quiet man was taking it all in: Beth and Alison, the tubes and breathing, the *Madonna and Child,* the quilt, and the puffiness.

Beth stirred and spoke to the quiet man. She spoke from the pain inside. She spoke from that hollow resonance of a wound that will never truly heal. She wanted answers. She needed answers. Answers, answers, my life, my everything, for answers.

"What has happened to my child? Why has this happened? What has caused this?" Quiet, quietness.

Beth spoke, "I feel betrayed. I was taught that when I pray to God that He hears my prayer, that He supports my life, that

God is there for me and my family. I have always prayed for my children. I have always been so grateful for my children. I have prayed and prayed for their safety and welfare. I had dreams of a tragedy and I turned to God. I do not feel He is here. Where is God?"

Quietly the man listened. He listened, and when he spoke he had the answers. He had the answers, all of the answers. He had taken it all in. He had the answers to all of Beth's questions.

He had the answer, the answer of patience. He had the answer, the answer of compassion. He had the answer, the answer of kindness. He had the answer, the answer of understanding. He had the answer, the answer of learning, of knowledge, and of experience. He had the one true answer, the answer of love. Yes, he had the answers, an arsenal of the greatest answers known to humankind. And he used them skillfully and artfully to answer the unanswerable and to bring into this doubt and death a breath of light and life. He answered all the questions that Beth asked, and Beth began to calm. She became reassured. She began to lift her heart from the depths of darkness. This was the first step in a long and difficult journey of healing.

Beth was then able to turn to more practical matters: the care of Alison's body, whether Thursday gave enough time for preparations for the funeral, and discussing her decision about organ donation. Rev. Dancey spent several hours with Beth going through her questions and concerns and orienting her for the next days and the haze of life ahead.

Beth had prayed for answers and guidance, and that is what she received. Such was the gift of a man of faith.

EARLY MORNING

When I awoke before sunup, the angels had stopped their singing and playing and the Word of God had been spoken. It was quiet. The priest had come and gone like a spirit in the night, dispensing wisdom and solace in the silence, making way for the approach of the sun and the tumult of day.

Beth was awake. She had been resting and dozing since the priest left. It was still dark. The machines beeped and buzzed and hummed and chortled right along. They served their master: life or lack of it was no concern to them. Alison was continuing to take on more fluids and was puffy, not even looking so much like herself. It was indeed the shell of the girl we knew, having presence even in death, but lacking that incredible vitality.

"I think Alison has moved on," I said.

Beth had been intertwined with Alison and wrapped in the love that they shared. She had not truly looked at Alison for some time. This forced her to look intently at Alison, and she suddenly saw that it was time to let go of Alison the body, and recognize that the Alison she loved was in the realm of spirit.

Beth and I spent some time in quiet meditation. The nurses would come through occasionally, but it was a peaceful time. Soon the noisy machines would be turned off and their false indications of life would be pulled from Alison's body.

Morning began to break on another beautiful day. The black of the sky gave way to dark blue; a beautiful orange glow appeared on the buildings as they caught fire from the first full rays of the sun. The city was beginning to stir.

Some of the life support bells and whistles were turned off. There was no longer a need for emergency response. It seemed strange that in the beauty of this dawn, of this beginning, we should have a finale. As morning came on, Charity and Kay joined us and the angels came, Sandi and Sheila, bleary-eyed from the little sleep they had gotten, but more than ready for the tasks at hand. In a very unceremonious way, the life support devices were removed, and yet there was no reaction. No physical change came over her, nothing. All was quiet.

Death is not extinguishing the light. It is putting out the Lamp because the Dawn has come.

– Tagore

Stephie awoke in the middle of that night to a shriek in her dreams — a shriek that she could only attribute to a mother losing her child. It woke her completely and she lit a candle and prayed. Several hours later, around the time when the life support was being removed from Alison, her candle flickered and sputtered and then returned to an even flame.

I am standing upon the seashore. A ship at my side spreads her white sails to the morning breeze and starts for the blue ocean. She is an object of beauty and strength and I stand and watch her until at length she hangs like a speck of white cloud just where the sea and sky come down to mingle with each other. Then someone at my side says: "There! She's gone."

Gone where? Gone from my sight — that is all. She is just as large in mast and hull and spar as she was when she left my side, and just as able to bear her load of living freight to the place of destination. Her diminished size is in me, not in her; and just at the moment when someone at my side says, "There! She's gone," there are other eyes watching her coming and other voices ready to take up the glad shout, "There she comes!

— Author Unknown

Alison on her 7th birthday: July 27, 1995

where the heart is

GOING HOME

After sunrise, after the life support was removed, Alison was given a sponge bath on her bed. Her hospital garment and the ripped remains of the shirt she had been wearing were taken off. Philamina helped Beth and the women as they undressed her and brought in towels, warm water, and soap. Her skin was bruised in many places from the IVs and she had retained fluid as well. Her neck brace was removed and the red scrape was quite large.

The women asked if I wanted to help, but I was not able to do more than a token amount. It was too painful for me to participate;

the finality of Alison's passing was brought home in this simple act of devotion and preparation. I thought of Mary tending Christ after the crucifixion. I could not imagine anything more difficult for a mother. I stood at the bedside stroking Alison but letting the women do their work of cleaning and preparing, bringing out beauty where I found only sorrow.

When Alison had been bathed, Beth asked for clothing for her. Peggy was only able to come up with baby hospital garments and Beth did not want them for Alison. Instead, Beth gave Alison her shirt. She was wearing a camisole, a shirt, and a sweater, and she took off her sweater and shirt. With the help of her friends who propped Alison up, Beth dressed Alison in her long flowing shirt and prepared her for her last journey home.

I left to make phone calls regarding arrangements. When I returned, the hospital bed had been wheeled from the room and the nurses had found a rocking chair for Beth. She had Alison on her lap with Sheila and Sandi taking turns holding Alison's legs. There was time available and Beth spent it quietly with Alison.

Beth had been at the hospital almost two days without eating and had left Alison only for short bathroom breaks although there were friends and family that wanted to help her with whatever could be done. The problem was that there was nothing to be done, or more accurately, nothing that could be done. The time with Alison on her lap was precious and all that she could ask for under the circumstances. It would take some time for her appetite to return and much, much longer for her interest in life to do so.

The time with Alison continued, but the attendants sent by the funeral home had not arrived. A man and a woman finally showed up almost two hours late. The man did the driving and lifting, and the woman's job was to work on the presentation of the deceased. They had gotten lost and had been misdirected several times. The man was in a bad mood and wanted to get in, get Alison, and get out.

He put Alison in a heavy bag and he insisted on zipping the bag all the way up even though Beth requested that he leave Alison's face uncovered. He then laid her on the gurney that they had brought upstairs. They left the ward with us following them and got on an elevator ahead of us. They were tearing down the basement hallway toward the exit when we finally caught up with them. We had a quick discussion and he was more helpful, but our hands-on approach to death was disconcerting for him. Beth would have ridden in the back of their van with Alison if he had allowed it.

We drove right behind them on the forty-five minute trip to Beth's house. It was the last time we saw the male attendant; our interactive approach was too much for him.

BETH'S HOME

When we were close to Beth's house, I pulled over and had the van stop behind me. I told the man that I wanted to scout things out. If the boys were home I did not want them to see us carrying Alison inside. We arrived at the house around noon and the boys were playing at a neighbor's home.

Beth's home is a two-story, Cape Cod–style dwelling built in the 1920s. It has ivy growing over most of the front of the house. Over the previous summer some ivy started creeping through an open window into the living room. Rather than cut it, Beth decided to train it inside the house on the curtain rod hanging at the top of double windows. The ivy gave a comfortable and inviting feel to all who entered the house.

We brought Alison into the living room on the gurney and prepared to bring her upstairs. The house was clean and welcoming, yet there was also a sadness to it. I felt it in the furniture, the couch looked sad to me, and the chair was drooping a bit. Even the walls looked sad.

We brought the casket, a beautiful and simple pine box, up to Alison's room. Then John Knox, Beth, and I carried Alison upstairs. I fought back my emotions as I knew this was the last time I would carry Alison to her room. She was placed in the casket with dry ice to keep her cool. The casket was placed sideways across the middle of her bed and supported by a chair at its head on the far side of the bed. In this position, visitors could sit on both the head and foot of the bed for prayer or to spend time with Alison. It was a comfortable and intimate setting.

Beth was not sure what she should have Alison wear. She was torn between two choices, a soft white dress with a pink border, or shorts, a polo shirt, and her Yankees baseball cap. It was a difficult choice since Alison was equally at home in either. She was both a tomboy and a little lady. Beth finally decided on the dress for Alison with a flower wreath in her hair and a garland around her neck over the red-scraped skin. Beth with the help of her mother dressed Alison with loving care.

The effect of the open casket upon all who visited Alison was profound. Anyone could come see her, touch her, have time with her, see the changes in her body, and recognize that her soul no longer had residence there. For the children especially, being with Alison was important, feeling at home with Alison and having time with their friend was a valuable life experience. Alison's temporal body underscored the mystery and fragility of earthly life.

BODY AND SOUL

Lark had been home that Tuesday making preparations for Alison's funeral. She was organizing the service, music, and the many details. She had kept her children home from school. Her four-year-old, Ethan, was around her, not getting too far from the center of activity. She was doing her research to provide Beth with as much information as possible.

Lark was talking to various people. She kept referring to "Alison's body," where it was, where it was going, how it was getting there. Her son started pulling at her arm. She continued her phone conversation trying to soothe him. He kept tugging.

She put her hand over the receiver as her arm was yanked. "Ethan, what is it?!"

His eyes were bright and wide.

"But, Mommy! Alison is right here! Can't you see her?!"

MOURNING CELEBRATION

Alison's room was wonderfully made up and the house was in order. All had been prepared for the grieving and celebrating ahead. Beth had consulted with me about the hours for visitation and how open the invitation should be for individuals, families, and children. We both came to the conclusion several times, as choices had to be made, that we wanted to include *all* who wanted to participate. We knew that Alison would love having as many people as possible. Alison loved a party, loved people, and loved being the center of attention. Therefore, everyone was encouraged to come. Beth and I also believed that this openness would bring its own sense of harmony, and that things would work out for the best. Visiting hours were from 3 to 9 P.M. that Tuesday and noon to 9 P.M. on Wednesday.

People started coming over to the house early, bringing food, support, and love. The table started filling up, the house started filling up, flower arrangements were being delivered. We would read the cards and be uplifted. At one point, Faith came to me in tears with a card in her hand. It simply read, "Our hearts are broken." It was from my parents and it captured the essence of what so many of us experienced. I cried too, and we hugged each other.

Beth's father, John Knox, kept asking Beth what she was going to do next as she was attending to details. "What next?" "Then what?" She kept on doing things and he was nearby. After a number of details had been handled and some arrangements made, he was again asking her what she was going to do. When she told him that she was going to take a bath, he was finally satisfied.

"That's just what you need," he said. "I was waiting to hear you say that."

Beth took a bath — a very, very long bath. Lark was in with her, going over ideas and plans for the funeral service. Beth needed to decide on readings, hymns, timing, and other details. Also, a number of people had volunteered to perform music at the service. I would pop in occasionally with a question or to pass on information. At one time, Beth's friend Camilla came in with her two daughters to give a gift to Beth. Beth was unabashedly holding court in the bath. Unique situations call for unique solutions and Beth resurfaced eventually in her bathrobe fresh from the bath to say good-bye to one of Rob's relatives and my parents, who were leaving the house.

Next, I took a shower and found that I had no fresh clothing, only what I had been wearing the last three days. I put on the same shorts and thought I should have something nicer. In the meantime, there were two shirts Beth had that I liked: one with flowers that reminded me of Alison, and a Nature Conservancy shirt with a big wolf face on the front. This also reminded me of Alison. I chose the wolf shirt and spent the entire day in that shirt and my shorts with no shoes (perhaps I should have worn one of Alison's baseball caps as well!) I thought Alison would appreciate it. Like Beth, I took into consideration what Alison would want in this situation. If I felt Alison would like it, that was very important to me. The next day someone was able to go to my house and pick up less casual clothing.

In the early afternoon, things got into high gear. There was a steady stream of food, people, flowers, children, older folks, deliveries, crying, embraces, coffee, laughter, family, tears, flowers, condolences, cookies, friends, cards, desserts, hugs, fruit, pasta, bouquets, infants, chicken, roses, laughter, children, juice, shouts, cake, hand-holding, pies, tears, acquaintances, tea, soda, embraces, flowers, salad, cards, hugs, and on and on.

Upstairs it was the same, but yet different. The vigil was kept in Alison's room. One or two people would be reading spiritual literature, praying, or meditating every moment with Alison. The vigil is designed as a positive flow of love and energy to help the soul in its transition from the physical earth to a new life in spirit. A chair and lamp were set aside in the room.

There were also people coming for a visit with Alison or wanting to see Beth, who spent as much time as possible in Alison's room. There were children coming through, the first time perhaps with trepidation, but afterwards feeling completely at home, not off-limits, not bizarre, not even unusual, it was just the room where Alison was. And then a new person would start the vigil and someone would come to meditate, another would come to spend time with Alison, and someone would come to give Beth support, another would bring her five-year-old to say good-bye to his or her close friend, and the mother would pass on a story to Beth from the child of something memorable that Alison had done. Perhaps Alison had given them something, or had this idea, or had done this brave act, or had created this fun game, or helped when this had happened, or had bested this strong person, or had sacrificed something of herself for others. And then someone else was reading for the vigil and several people were on the bed and a new child wanted to see her friend, and someone else came to pray, and a couple meditated in a corner, and a relative shared a moment with Beth.

The room drew people in. There were tears and hugs and kisses and laughter and flowers and stories and silence and hand-holding and prayer...and food just like downstairs except spiritual food of communion with each other, within ourselves, and through reading, prayer, meditation, and contemplation. The bread of life was broken and we all gave because we had been given, and we all ate because we needed to eat. Everyone in their own way added and shared in this.

So it went downstairs, upstairs, outside, and in the basement. Things continued up and down, here and there, in the house and outside the house, through the house and around the house, children, parents, relatives, friends, toddlers, games, conversation, food, tag, drinks, trampoline, football, toys.

John and Sue Knox left to return to Syracuse. They would be back early Thursday before the funeral service. "After all, it's only seven hours," they said. They were picking up Beth's brother, Sam, in Syracuse as well; he was flying in from Phoenix and wanted time with them. They also had horses to feed and animals to tend to — and the drive was only seven hours.

When everyone had left by 11 P.M., there was still much to do, organizing, airport pick-ups, details, details. Several hundred people had stopped by, and somewhere in the midst of all this activity, somehow, the house had lost its unhappiness and there was a feeling of warmth and love. By 3 A.M. things had slowed enough for bed.

A STAR IS BORN

At the end of the first day at Beth's home, a green star-shaped box with a lovely ribbon arrived. Beth sent this note to the school newsletter shortly after:

> "Every day new stars are discovered in the heavens. A star discovered on October 15, 1995 has been named in honor of Alison. The star will be known as the Alison Crocker Sanders star.
>
> Now whenever the children and their parents are afraid or sad, or filled with happiness they want to share, look up to the Heavens. The brightest star shining and twinkling is Alison's, and she sends her light, love and laughter to comfort us."
>
> These words arrived in a star-shaped box to Alison's home. We do not officially know who arranged this wonderful memorial, but we thank them from the depths of our hearts. We share this knowledge with you so that you can feel the joy that we felt.
>
> Alison's star can be found in the Ursa Major (Great Bear) constellation whose coordinates are RA: 9h 38m 43s D: 44° 13' for you astronomers!

WEDNESDAY

At 8 A.M. on Wednesday the day began. The day started overcast. As I came out into the living room, there it was again — the lonely chair in the corner, and now that I noticed it, the couch was looking a little down too, and the walls, yes, well, I am sure they couldn't help it. The house was sad again — feeling the loss just like we were.

Soon the phone started ringing with information and questions on details and scheduling. Afterward, I played football with the boys outside. Pumpkin the cat had put up with the crowds and children and was enjoying the quiet house. The boys' cousin, Ryan, and Beth's brother, Randy, would be arriving this day. Good friends and family were expected as well.

Around 9:30, women from the school started to arrive with more food and drinks for the day. By 10:30 people were starting to drop in for a quick visit, or because this was the only time they could come by, or to ask if there was anything we needed.

So it began again, the Great Visitation. The funeral director sent an attendant with more dry ice to put around Alison. She was packed in and cool to the touch. A condolence book was brought over and placed on a beautiful pedestal. People were encouraged to share memories and thoughts of Alison; magic markers were available for children to draw pictures. It was a big hit and has since become a valued keepsake for the family.

Everything was condensed. Decisions that one would want to mull over were made in a snap. The funeral service was constructed: music, chorus, and prayers. Alison was to be cremated. This was to be done right after the service about a half-hour drive from the church. Only family would be attending a short service before the cremation. All had to be discussed, rendered, and effected in compressed time. I spent the whole day organizing something, actually a number of somethings.

Wednesday was a carbon copy of the day before, but longer. Less flowers arrived and more people came through. The weather turned beautiful in the afternoon. There were also more children and they were playing on the trampoline in great numbers. This became somewhat regulated, but there were many children roaming about at any time, in the basement playing, outside playing guns or tag games, running through the house, up to see Alison for a time, and then outside for another round of screaming-crazies. Matthew and David were thrilled to have all of their friends over to the house, staying up very late, and having friends and family come for a visit. Yes, and we knew that Alison loved it, too. It was life at full throttle. What strange things come out of such events!

The day continued, built up a head of steam, got going full bore, and raced on and on. The sun was bright and warm. A courier showed up with a beautiful picture of Alison that he had picked up from Rob and Lyn's house in Baltimore.

Beth had taken the picture at her mother's beach house. It had been twilight and there were kites flying in the air. Matthew, David, and Alison jumped and pranced about on the beach enjoying the spectacle. A beautiful light glowed everywhere and Beth went to get her camera. When she came back, Alison was lying in the sand gazing up. Beth looked through the viewfinder and clicked, and she knew that this would be an extraordinary picture. She started snapping away getting many wonderful shots of the children. Later, when the film was developed, she and the children opened the envelope. The close-up of Alison gazing up got exclamations from everyone. "Guys! Don't I look grown up?!" she said. Beth gave one print to Alison's grandmother, Faith, and one print to Rob. Beth had mailed off the negative for more prints the week before the accident and they had not come back.

I took one look at this picture of Alison on the beach staring up into the heavens and burst into tears. It captured Alison's spirit wonderfully. Every time I saw that picture in the ensuing days I was moved to tears. Once I was telling someone about this and proceeded to pull out my copy of the picture to show it to him — big mistake!

Beth's cousins, the Turners, showed up at 6 P.M. They had all packed into the car for the journey down from Connecticut. It was great to see them. It was a relief to have Beth's family present and to feel their support. Late in the afternoon, John and Sue Knox made their mysterious reappearance from Syracuse, "Just seven hours away," with Sam. They were not supposed to return until the following day, the day of the funeral, but their competence and know-how were needed. Besides it was the place they should be.

The house was packed, the upstairs was full, children were everywhere. Yes, this indeed must be a celebration of Alison's. The hugging, pain, kissing, crying, laughing, loss, smiling, touching, playfulness, and heartache were all too much. The evening wore on and the dads who had not been around began to show up. Rob's family was present in full force. I was meeting cousins, uncles, aunts, sort-of-cousins, and marriage and blood relations who all had the same four last names.

Everyone spoke highly of Rob, "How is he? Where is he? Will he be all right? This could have easily have happened to me.... Our love and prayers are with him.... We're all rooting for him." There was much love and concern directed toward him.

Beth's main focus was spending as much time with Alison as possible, and sometimes this was not possible. Decisions and responsibilities brought her, sometimes drove her, from that meditative environment where Alison's body resided. She could get caught in the kitchen for an hour going from one person to the next, always ostensibly on her way upstairs.

FURTHER REVIEW

John Knox is a big man. Six feet, seven inches in his prime, and now at 65 an inch or so shorter. Weighing about 235 pounds with a strong presence, sometimes intimidating, he has mellowed tremendously with age. He is an engineer and proud of it, used to solving problems by the correct application of intelligence, trial and error, and tenacity. He had built up a lifetime of experience, was self-sufficient with Yankee know-how, and when he had an opinion or fact, he would speak it. He had a way of getting on a problem, sinking his teeth into it, and not letting go until there was a satisfactory conclusion. He would look at something in as many ways as necessary until the problem, its mechanics, and solution revealed themselves. Getting by was not good enough.

John had heard a news report about a young boy who was apparently killed by an air bag in a low-speed accident in Utah. There was another report of a similar child fatality as well. He started wrapping his mind around Alison's death in his vise-like way. The result was a question, "What was the physical cause of death for Alison?"

"Wonderful!" I thought. "This is wonderful! Twelve hours before the funeral and we are calling all over creation trying to find doctors at Johns Hopkins who can give us an accurate cause of death. Twelve hours before the funeral and we may be scheduling an autopsy and holding up this whole process. Twelve hours before the funeral and we are not sure whether to cremate Alison or look more closely for a missing link."

I was not about to talk to Beth about this. The whole plan for completion was being jeopardized by a left-brained Yankee engineer. But John did not raise questions to cause trouble and stir things up (though this was often the result!), he raised them to get to a deeper level of understanding. As my desire was to tie everything up as neatly as possible and get on with things, his desire was to put things in their proper place before laying them to rest. If this meant not laying them to rest in their prescribed place at the prescribed time, so be it! The question was put to Beth and, to my surprise, she was willing to explore this issue. Jane, Kay, and I spent hours on the phone trying to answer this question, and it was impossible to tell where the truth lay. Finally, we got a doctor on the line from the pediatric ward who would speak only to Beth, and so Beth came down from Alison's room. Beth put her concerns before the doctor and they had a long talk.

Fundamentally he left her with two messages: "First, don't let your family pressure you into getting an autopsy performed, and second, if you think it was the air bag that killed your daughter, you could spend years of your life and a great deal of money fighting this in courts and possibly come away with nothing." He had seen situations where the auto industry would fight tooth and nail and never give an inch. He felt that Beth would only be taking on a mountain of aggravation with no reward.

Beth was relieved that this situation did not seem worth pursuing any further; the last thing she wanted was an autopsy performed on her daughter in some useless exercise. She had followed up to the best of her ability and now things should take their course. After all, weren't air bags a safety device, designed to save lives? Wasn't this all a result of inattention on Rob's part? This seemed like an overreaction by an over-cerebral Yankee bulldog. Perhaps John Knox was just trying to bring meaning to this mystery and find an explanation that would bring some solace to his family. Or was there something more here, some silent missing piece to the tragedy, a design flaw hidden underneath the human error? Can't we just bury this whole thing, I thought, and put it all to rest? Maybe other people unknown to us were hoping we would do just that.

Perhaps there are simply things that cannot be laid to rest and silences that people keep that are quieter than death.

⁀

This night, the last night, Beth slept upstairs with Alison. She curled up at the head of the bed next to the casket. Pumpkin slept on the opposite side of Alison at the foot of the bed. Beth stayed there from 3 A.M. through the night with the vigil-keepers coming and going.

⁀

ANGEL OF MY SWEET DREAMS

(Sung in the pentatonic scale;
a bedtime song adapted by Beth and Alison
from Mother of the Fairy Tale*)*

Angel of my sweet dreams,

Take me by your silver hand,

Take me in your silver boat,

Sail me silently afloat.

Angel of my sweet dreams,

Take me to your shining land.

69

touching the light

Dear Beth,

I don't think I have told you how grateful I am to you for opening your heart and home to those whose pain is so much less than yours. I feel as though you and Alison gently led us through the valley of the shadow of death and showed us that we should fear no evil. I have learned more from you in a week than a lifetime of schooling had taught. I have learned that there can be no life without death, that death is intensely painful for the living but that it is not itself evil. I have learned lessons about love and caring and hope.

I am also deeply grateful for your inclusion of the children particularly at your home. You taught a school full of children about death and life and love — lessons that in subtle ways will transform their lives.

Alison will dwell in our hearts forever. We have all been changed by her life and by her death. Thank you for the love and lessons you have shared.

Love,

Wendy Perdue

(Beth's carpool partner)

RIDING HIGH

Alison did not learn to ride a bike early. In fact, it took her quite a while to learn, but this had more to do with inclination than anything else. Beth had the baby seat on her bike for Alison as well as to carry groceries, bags of apples, and to do errands for work. Alison enjoyed looking at the world, taking things in, and generally having a meditative view while being chauffeured about. There was no hurry to learn to ride a bike, and by the time she did learn, she was like a giant in the tiny baby seat with her big legs bunched up pressing into her stomach. The bike she learned to ride on was little and served as a poor mode of transportation.

One day in late September, Beth called at the end of my workday to see if I could join her and the children for a ride before dinner. I told her to meet me at a street corner on the way down to the park. I showed up at the appointed time and they were nowhere to be seen. Finally, Beth and her brood arrived. I saw two little helmeted heads approaching very tentatively on bikes. Behind them, Beth and Alison came, Beth yelling commands to all three, keeping them in order and not wandering into the middle of the street.

We started on a ride and after ten minutes Matthew was huffing and puffing. I took his bike to test drive the gears and found that it only rode in lower gears. He was working at least twice as hard as the rest of us to go the same distance!

Toward the end of the ride, on the way back up the half-mile incline to Beth's house, Alison's legs finally gave out. Her little bike was not built for easy riding and she was tired. Beth went ahead with the boys, and Alison and I brought up the rear. I told Alison that I was not sure what to do because I had two bikes to take plus her. We then tried to fit her bike on my bike and leave enough room for both of us. After a number of attempts I told her that I did not think we could do it.

"Well," she said, "Jane Parker did it."

"Oh!" I thought, "Well if Jane can do it…"

So I determined to make it work. I put the bike partially over the handlebars and held it with my left hand. She got on the seat with her feet sticking out away from the spokes and off we went with me half-sitting, pedaling as best as I could up the long meandering hill.

"Well," she said, as though she was just coming to think of it, "Jane and I were going downhill."

"Oh!" I thought again.

She asked if we could go up the steepest route when we got to a fork in the road. This would actually take us a bit above Beth's house and was extra work for me, but I consented. We got to the steep section and I was pedaling hard as we went up, thinking that it would be an accomplishment for me to best the hill with Alison and her bike aboard.

When we got up nearly to the top of the hill Alison said, "Okay, Okay! Let me down!" I was not finished with my goal of getting to the top, but I did as I was asked. She got off.

"My feet are killing me!" she continued, walking off the stiffness from holding her legs rigidly out. "Now," she said in full control, "let me have my bike. I want to ride down the hill to our house."

"Oh!" I thought again as I gave her the bike. I went ahead of her so she could enjoy the hill without interruption of traffic. She came down with concentration and presence if not great form, enjoying, I believe, her mastery over both gravity and man!

HALLOWEEN SCARECROW

The week before the accident, while driving home from school, Alison told Beth that she wanted to make a scarecrow. It was weeks before Halloween, but she felt strongly about doing it. Beth gathered materials for Alison but did not help with the enterprise. Alison stuffed dark clothing with newspaper since there was no hay available. She also had an ugly monster mask that she used for the face. When she had finished, Beth sat it in a living room chair waiting for Halloween. Alison had done it, she had created a truly ugly scarecrow!

The day that Alison was brought home from the hospital and laid in her room, Beth went into the basement late in the afternoon to talk to her boys among the roving groups of children. Her eyes fell on an ugly scarecrow tucked into a corner, still waiting for Halloween. Beth's heart sank and a cry of anguish came forth.

Often it is the simplest remembrance that touches us most deeply in our grief.

—

Do not stand at my grave and weep.
I am not there. I do not sleep.
I am a thousand winds that blow.
I am the diamond glints on snow.
I am the sunlight on ripened grain.
I am the gentle autumn rain.
When you awake in the morning's hush
I am the soft uplifting rush
Of quiet birds in circling flight.
I am the soft star that shines at night.
Do not stand at my grave and cry.
I am not there.
I did not die.

– Anonymous

TOUCHING THE LIGHT

The letter below was written by Kay Knox's fiancee:

Beth, Pat, David, and Matthew,

I wanted to write to you all and convey my deepest sympathy to you all on the loss of your Alison. She was a very special girl and will be greatly missed by all that knew and loved her.

I also wanted to share with you all a memory from this summer. It's a memory of a short period of time that Alison and I spent at the beach. Alison wanted to go visit the lighthouse and no one was around except for me, so I was elected. As we climbed the endless stairs to the top of the lighthouse we looked out the windows on the way. Alison was pointing out the landmarks to me as we went. She was quite knowledgeable about the lighthouse and I was surprised.

When we got to the top we were able to look out in all directions and see for many miles. Alison really enjoyed this part and kept scurrying around the circular platform at the top. While we were up there she noticed the little light at the end of the jetty and matter-of-factly decided she wanted to go there and touch it. So off we went.

We went back down the endless stairs and finally made it back to the bottom. As we were walking out on the jetty, Alison commented that it looked a lot closer from the top of the lighthouse than it did from the ground, and I agreed. I then asked if she wished to continue and she said yes. We were just about halfway there at that time. While we were walking to the end, Alison was leading the way and told me to follow her as best as I could because she knew the correct way. I said I would follow as best as I could. She was moving very quickly and it was a chore to keep up with her.

Once we reached the section of the jetty that extends out into the water we noticed that the waves were crashing into the rocks and sending ocean spray all over the place. Again I asked Alison if she wished to continue and she determinedly said yes. She wanted to touch the light at the end. We had to dodge numerous waves that crashed into the rocks on that final leg to the end, but we made it. Both of us were a little wet when we got there, and there were a couple of boys there doing some fishing. We admired their catch and then Alison climbed the little ladder to the light and touched it. She wanted me to touch it also, so I did. We accomplished our goal of making it to the end and touching the light!

I'm going to choose to remember Alison from this day we went to the end of the jetty. I'll remember her for her spirit of adventure. I'll remember her for her curiosity on the way. I'll remember her for her knowledge of her surroundings. I'll remember her for determination to make it to the end. I'll remember her for her sense of invincibility to the elements. I'll remember her for the joy she exuded while she was skipping over the rocks on the way to the end. But most of all I'll remember her for the fun we had that day on our trip to touch the light at the end of the jetty.

Sincerely and with love,
Brian Thompson

A CHILD'S STORY

The Thursday night before the accident, Alison wanted to share a story she had learned in school that day. Alison was an excellent storyteller, however, she sometimes had the gift of the gab and went on too long. She told us it was a long story, so we agreed to hear half of the story that night and the other half after the children spent the weekend with their father.

Alison had heard the story accompanied by gestures and movement. She told us that she would tell the story with accompanying movements as well.

The story was about a girl who kept losing herds of animals in her care to an evil sorcerer. The sorcerer would disguise himself as an animal in the woods and would feign illness or pain. The girl would help the distressed animal while the sorcerer contrived to steal away the herd in the girl's care. Eventually the girl learned the sorcerer's secrets. She went to great lengths to recover the animals and prevent the sorcerer from employing his evil tricks.

As Alison told the story, she used common hand gestures for emphasis. Matthew asked if these were the movements that Alison said she would use. Beth and I laughed as it was obvious that remembering the story line and telling it was hard enough for Alison. Her hand movements were part of her natural expression.

Although Alison had heard it only once, the story was interesting and told well. We enjoyed it and listened all the way through to the end. We were proud of Alison and applauded her. She was proud of her accomplishment as well and went to bed beaming that night.

ALISON AT DINNER

Alison is sitting at the kitchen table finishing her dinner and turns to me: "I love, love, love," now her fork is jabbing in the air, "Love, love, love," her body rocking to the rhythm, "Love, love," a smile growing on her face, "Love, love," her eyes twinkling, "Love youuuu!"

Out of breath, and now the full happy face smile!

PALL BEARERS

Earlier in the day on Wednesday, Beth was in the kitchen discussing funeral arrangements. She was asked who she wanted as pall bearers. She thought for a moment.

"I'd like to have my father (6' 7"), and brothers Sam (6' 2") and Randy (6' 3"), my cousin Flip (6' 2"), and close friend John White (6' 3"), and Pat (5' 10")."

Somehow, when she got to me, and the height difference between me and everyone else, it struck Beth as comical. She could see this short guy with hands held high trying to support the coffin.

"I guess Pat will just have to do this!" Beth said, and began prancing about the kitchen with her hands over her head, palms up, imitating me trying to support a coffin high above. Everyone was a little amazed at Beth's spontaneity and humor, and enjoyed a good laugh.

"Pat, squeeze me as hard as you can."

"Okay, Alison." I grab her. "Hrrrrmph!"

"No, Pat! I want you to squeeze me as hard as you can."

"Here we go!! — How was that?"

"Pat, I want you to squeeze me with all your might!"

"Alison, if I did that, I'd hurt you."

"Paaat! Please!! Squeeze me hard!" So I grab her and start applying more force slowly, then more pressure, and a little more — now she is starting to get uncomfortable — and a little more. Her face is beginning to turn red. And a little more. And —

"Okay, let go!" she takes a big breath and looks me in the eye. "Was that as hard as you could?"

"Alison, that was pretty hard!"

She reflects for a moment.

"Okay. Now sit on me with all your weight."

KEEPERS OF THE WATCH

In the letter below, Lark Bergwin-Anderson listed those who kept the around-the-clock vigil with Alison and their schedules:

October 24, 1995

Dearest Beth, Matthew and David,

I thought that you might like to have the list of those who shared such a special time with Alison by keeping vigil with her.

There were many others who also expressed a desire to sit but I ran out of time slots, so these are the lucky ones. Every *single* vigil keeper with whom I have spoken has conveyed to me what a sacred time it was, how that Time, like Alison herself, will be carried with them. She is a very special individual, and her Threshold Crossing has forever changed this community who love her and you all so well.

You are in my heart,

Lark

Beth with Matthew, David, and Alison: Summer, 1994

show time

CLOSING CEREMONIES

Beth arose early to start the day. There were still many preparations to be made for the funeral. We were also going to tape record the service for Rob. We had hoped that he could make it, but it was not possible.

Rev. Dancey had kept the vigil from 3 to 5 A.M. and was at the house in the morning. At 11 A.M., the family gathered upstairs for the closing of the casket. About twenty of us gathered in Alison's room. Beth, Matthew, and David sat at the head and foot of the bed and I came over to comfort Beth. The rest of us stood in the crowded space.

Then suddenly, just as we were getting settled, "Our Father," Rev. Dancey began, "Who art in heaven," the timing was perfect, "hallowed be Thy name," and drew us into the moment. "Thy Kingdom come, Thy will be done," our pain and suffering were exposed, "on earth as it is in Heaven. Give us this day our daily bread," we felt the incongruity of this mystery, "but forgive us our trespasses, as we forgive those who trespass against us." We were unified, one thought, one voice, "and lead us not into temptation, but deliver us from evil." We spoke in supplication, humbled, "for Thine is the kingdom and the power and the Glory. Amen."

The ordered Universe, the Power behind it, and our small but profound connection were revealed. The prayer was finished and it was time to close the casket. John Knox put the first half of the pine top on and I put the other half on in Rob's name. Beth placed a single pink sweetheart rose on top and her father secured the stem between the halves of the lid.

After the women left, a group of men picked up the coffin and began to carry it downstairs. It was quite heavy and we maneuvered it gingerly down the stairs while keeping it level. We then carried Alison out to the hearse.

We rode in a procession of about ten vehicles to the church. There was a long line at the church entrance because people were signing a book of remembrances for the family. We waited a few minutes and then hustled everyone inside so seats could be taken. I wore a bright blue tie with flowers for Alison.

Alison embodied truth, beauty, wisdom, compassion, love, integrity, honesty, strength, humor, and courage. I felt that she had graduated from this earthly life to a place of light and love, and that this was truly a celebration.

⌐

Dear Beth,

I wanted to thank you for the profound gift you have given this community by choosing to have Alison's wake and receiving at your home! I have been to funerals which have been *so* awkward at funeral parlors.

The experience at your house with Alison upstairs in the bedroom was amazing. It was profoundly moving and real.

I have been to several home births and the evening at your house reminded me very much of those times. We were together to honor a passage from one realm to another — sadly back to a place we can only see in our dreams — but still so similar. My deepest love to you as you take up your life again.

Barbara

✍

ORDER OF SERVICE

Alison Crocker Sanders
July 27,1988~October 15,1995

The sun in your heart shall glow,
The stars round your head shall sound,
The moon shall uphold from below
The earth shall give firm ground
Holding up high your head,
Stretching your hands out wide
Your feet shall surely tread
With the Grace of God to Guide
– Rev. Evelyn Capel

✍

Beth, Matthew, David, and Blossom walked slowly up the aisle to the first pew. Beth carried "Princess Blossom Bride," as named by Alison, a beautiful handwork doll that Beth had made for her. Alison had loved Blossom. Beth had Alison's baby doll to hold and comfort her through the service, a doll that Beth would keep close thereafter as a remembrance of her baby. When they were seated, the pall bearers carried Alison to the front of the church.

The church was full to overflowing with seven hundred people gathered for the service. Preludes were performed by Tria, a fifth-grader in Matthew's class, on harp, and by Nicholas, a high school violinist, who played "Ave Maria." Three lyre players performed in the service. Hymns were sung by those assembled including "All Things Bright and Beautiful." The high school chorus sang "Ave Verum" by Mozart. Rev. Dancey gave this eulogy:

> Dear Beth, Matthew, and David,
> Dear family,
> Dear relatives of Alison,
> Dear friends:
>
> Once there was a girl with a big problem. Although she looked small, she had a great fire inside. Alison's fire was bright and as strong as the sun. The name of that fire was love, all-embracing love. With that fire inside she wanted to be with all the people she loved all the time. She wanted to wrap her arms around all of you. But how could she? They were here and there and everywhere. No matter how far and wide she could stretch her arms they could only go so far.
>
> She wanted to be with her mother. She wanted to be with her father who lived in a different place. She wanted to be with her brothers, with all of her classmates, with her grandparents, her uncles and aunts, particularly with her grandmother who had died a tragic death. She wanted to be with so many. She wanted to be with them all, not just a quick visit, moving here and there, stirring around like a squirrel in the forest, but all the time. Like guardian angels are with us all of the time — that was her greatest, her deepest desire. She wanted to be actually more than a guardian angel. She wanted to be more like an archangel, watching over, standing, helping so many,

many people, like the sun that stands and watches over plants and animals and all the people around the whole earth all of the time every day. And how could she?

She could do what Alison has done. She could leave her body that was beautiful and strong, but small and not nearly as beautiful and strong and surely not nearly as great as that fire inside. She could set the fire free and go and be with Michael and with Michael be with them all.

I don't know whether Alison told me this story last night when I slept. It was here in the morning, in the early morning, when I awoke. I do not know if Alison told me the words that I now am going to say. But I know they have come into my heart to be said to you today.

Beth, Alison *is* your daughter; she loves you now as you love her. She will be with you and near you as you remember, and I pray you come to sense that with an open heart. And Robert, though Robert is not physically here, I say these words to him now and I will say them to him directly I hope, very soon. Robert, Alison *is* your daughter and she wants to and will be with you in this terrible time. Do not blame. Do not hate yourself, cast your stone. Love her, love her as she loves you, the two of you together. Matthew and David, Alison *is* your sister, your little sister but maybe also now your big sister. She is and will be your true companion for each of you the rest of your lives until you go to be with her. And that day will be a great day for her and for you. And to all of you, first grade classmates and friends, Alison *is* your great companion. She is and will be with you this year in Advent, in Christmas, in Easter and in the years ahead to the eighth and twelfth grade and beyond. For there is a bond now created, let it not be broken, forged in her dying by the fire of her love and good.

When you are dancing, she dances, when you sing, she sings, when you grow older and are facing life's

struggles and maybe dark nights, she will be there, with
the fire of her spirit burning warm and bright. In that
spirit we carry our questions and bring our prayers. We
turn to Alison, to Beings, to Michael, to Christ, in honor
and praise, in faith and hope and above it all, surrounding all, in all-embracing light of human life. Yea so be it!

The service came to a close, and as a pall bearer, I was concerned that I might be overwhelmed with grief. When we went to
pick up the casket, however, the love and support in the church
lifted me high. I felt honored to be among those with duties at
Alison's crossing and able to shoulder some of the burden. We carried Alison outside into the bright sunlight. We brought her to the
hearse and then spent time in the huge crowd, sharing the after-
glow from the service and living in the warmth of the moment.

Dear Beth,

At the service we sat in the balcony in a church
almost overflowing. We saw everybody there and St.
John's Church felt like a sacred place. Love was in the
air, as well as sadness and joy. There was a sense of
poignancy in that entire building which moved so many
of us to tears. Yes, we felt the absence of Rob and perhaps that added even more to the mood, to the farewells
and respects we mortals were paying to Alison.

It was also clear to me that there was a celebration
awaiting Alison in the Spiritual World, and I felt that she
was somehow echoed in the lyre and harp pieces. The
music was extraordinarily gentle and reassuring.

It was "out of the blue" and with great clarity that
Tria offered to play the harp. Her words were filled with
light and a desire for service to your family. Tria, too,
played from her heart and soul for Alison, who must
have helped her in return. It was uncanny how the notes

and sounds came through, as if it were a dialogue between Alison herself and us, and Tria was listening to Alison, to the harp, and to all the congregation that was supporting her.

The otherworldly quality stayed with me for weeks afterwards, and I will always carry this memory. When I caught a glimpse of you, I saw the most poised and yet vulnerable mother, grieving but also accepting. With such dignity and grace, you smiled through tears, and you walked forward, with Reverend Dancey's reminder to all of us, "Alison IS your daughter. Alison IS your sister. Alison IS your friend." Yes, she still is, and more than ever. This immensely powerful experience for all of us has been uplifting even though the temptation is to be dragged down.

I acknowledge the loss of words when it comes to a mother — who loved her daughter with all her body, heart, mind, soul, and more — losing her child. But I know that anymore when we see news of children dying and mothers grieving we will see the universal is also personal. They are one in the other.

Each holiday will be so difficult and new without Alison but I hope you take comfort in knowing that hundreds and hundreds of friends are sending you love and good thoughts. Alison is and will be with you, all your life.

With love and friendship,
E.F., Eddie, and Tria

THE CREMATORIUM

We finally got into vans and cars and prepared to go. We followed in a cavalcade from the church. Our spirits were uplifted by the service. The atmosphere had softened, and our mood was lighter. The children's cousins, Eli and Emily, joined us and I asked Eli what the last day had been like with Alison.

"We played football. We climbed trees. We were outside a lot playing games and having fun." He reflected for a second and then continued, "If I was gong to die, that's what I'd like my last day to be like!"

I could tell he meant it and I was filled with brightness at how fully Alison had lived — almost every day was like that — and how aware Eli was of life around him.

As we drove, I began to tell the story to the group in the van of the whole event as it had happened. I started by describing what Beth and I had done on Sunday and what a full day it had been, the news, how we reacted, what we did, everything of importance. The van wound its way off of the Washington Beltway and we turned into an industrial park. I continued on about arrivals and tidbits and comings and goings. I was retracing the last morning in the hospital as we pulled up in front of a nondescript building and got out. I broke off my story at that point and we entered a waiting room at the crematorium; all of the family and Rev. Dancey were present.

Rev. Dancey explained what was going to happen: we would go into a room with Alison; she would be on a cart out of the casket; we would have a few minutes with her, then there would be a prayer; finally, Alison would be put into the furnace chamber and we would leave.

It sounded straightforward enough. We proceeded down a short hallway into a well-lit, stark room, four cinder block walls painted gray with a concrete floor. Alison was on a rolling cart near the center of the room with a few of her stuffed animals and toys, including some wax figures that had been made by her schoolmates. She looked beautiful in her gown, lying like a sleeping angel. The swelling had subsided somewhat and she looked more herself. There was nothing else in the room. One of the walls had a metal door about three feet off the ground and about three feet square. Next to this was a control panel with knobs and dials. There was a man standing next to this panel in a white lab coat.

We gathered around Alison. This would be the last time we would see her. I came to her and kissed her on the forehead, that same round, full forehead I had kissed many times. It felt so familiar. A few other people came over to say good-bye. Faith kissed Alison and then broke down crying. Matthew, now taller than his grandmother, put his arm around her in comfort. This loving gesture brought unexpected smiles to our faces.

Beth's father, John, stood next to Beth and put his arm around her — facing the storm with her. They were standing next to Alison, and the cart she was on began to gently sway. Beth was moving it slowly back and forth with her foot, rocking her baby for the last time.

"The Lord is my shepherd," Rev. Dancey started the Twenty-third Psalm, again capturing that moment of pause and bringing us back to a place of true perspective, "I shall not want." We all joined in, "He maketh me to lie down in green pastures: He leadeth me beside the still waters. He restoreth my soul: He leadeth me in the paths of righteousness for His name's sake. Yea, though I walk through the valley of the shadow of death, I will fear no evil: for Thou art with me; Thy rod and Thy staff they comfort me. Thou preparest a table before me in the presence of mine enemies: Thou anointest my head with oil; my cup runneth over. Surely goodness and mercy shall follow me all the days of my life: and I will dwell in the house of the Lord for ever."

How perfectly these words surrounded us. We wrestled with the sweetness, the inescapable challenges of life, and this incomprehensible event laid out in front of us — mortality and spirit intertwined. How mortal we felt!

All was quiet. There was silence and the man in the lab coat turned on the oven and then walked over to Alison. He wheeled her up to the metal door. Most of the stuffed animals and toys were removed from the cart. Beth left a floppy-eared dog that Alison had had for years on the cart to go with her on her journey. Beth told the boys that they could go over to the panel for a look if they were curious. They did so in the few minutes it took for the oven to heat up.

The man opened the door and we could see the shadow of flame in the wall of the oven. It looked strangely like a movie prop. Then he got behind Alison and gave a shove to the board she was on. She slid inside the chamber and he shut the door. We stood in the room alone together.

Rev. Dancey came forward and stated that the service was over. We went out quietly to the waiting room. There were tears and hugs.

Matthew came up to his mother in the hallway, putting his arms around her and burying his face in her chest.

"Mommy, when is this going to be over?" is all he said.

We were subdued. We had been humbled. The finality was overwhelming. The ride back to the house was quiet.

Beth, however, had fulfilled what her heart had asked of her on Sunday evening: to be with her daughter every step of the way, every second of the time between learning of the accident and the final conclusion that was to come. This was not the conclusion that Beth desired, prayed for, and sought, but it was the conclusion that life had given her. Beth rose to this challenge with grace and dignity. She also acted with the thought of Alison's needs and welfare, and made all arrangements taking into consideration Alison's preferences.

Ultimately, Beth sought to acknowledge Alison's continuing spiritual life and, inevitably, was drawn to the Almighty Power behind this mystery of life and death. Here we had been witness to the final step in this whirlwind of transformation and the end of the physical bond that connected Alison to her family and friends. In this loss, however, Beth had created a living testament by the care with which Alison was honored and in the hearts and minds of those who had been touched by this event.

This event was a reflection of who Alison was in body and who she *is* in spirit as well — a positive legacy was created. The love and support were healing for family and friends, and propelled Alison forward in her continuing journey of spirit.

⇁

The Arabic word for death translates as "not here — present elsewhere."

Dear Beth, Matthew and David,

After the funeral — all I can think of is how Alison's fire burned us all. Burned us in a beautiful, thoughtful special way. Your little warrior has conquered all.

Everyone at the funeral was aglow with fire, warmth, and so much love.

What remains is the love. It feels like there is no call to hold onto it — it is there.

We are all with you.

Love, Sherry and family

SOCCER DAY

Gabe Schneider, a student at the Washington Waldorf School, was also in the same soccer league as Matthew and David. A week before the accident, his father, Ted, came to his son's soccer game. He saw Rob and came over to him.

"I see Matthew is playing," he said to Rob conversationally.

"And David, too!" a young voice boomed out of nowhere. Ted turned to a little girl half his height standing facing him.

"And David is playing, too!" she said again emphatically.

"Yes," Ted said looking onto the field but responding more to the emotional pressure being applied, "I see David is playing, too."

"Who is this?" he thought to himself. "Who is this angel of protection hovering around every word spoken about the boys on the field?"

"Who are you?" he said with interest, inclining his big frame, and warming to this large presence next to him housed in the body of a seven-year-old.

"I'm Alison," she said with authority, "and those are my brothers!"

BACK HOME

When we arrived at Beth's home, the late afternoon sun was low and strong, and the view to the west was blinding. There was a large group of people on the front lawn eating and drinking, enjoying the perfect evening. Although we had not been more than an hour behind the arrival of the guests at the house, everyone had settled in, eaten most of what was available, and was basking in the glow of the wonderful service. Again, many children were running, jumping, and playing. We had removed the trampoline from the backyard, placing it in a neighbor's yard (upside down) to keep the children out of harm's way.

Our mood was different than that of the people at the house. We were deflated after our experience at the crematorium, and all of the activity and the crowd seemed a bit much. What we wanted was peace and quiet. Beth said she might go upstairs to have some quiet time alone. Perhaps we should not have opened this up to such a large group. We wandered around, integrating ourselves into the crowd as best we could. Gradually things lightened up and we felt more at home.

There was a call for me and I went into the kitchen. It was Leslie Bloom, the woman for whom Beth worked. Leslie wrote a column on food in the *Washington Post*. She was in the throes of writing a cookbook and was an expert on fine food.

"Pat," she said, "my husband, David, and I are about to come over. What can we bring?"

"What can they bring?!" I said out loud to no one in particular. Drinks, bread, dessert, napkins — I was thinking of some minor item for them to bring.

"FOOD!" the answer came back from the women who had helped organize refreshments.

"Food. You can bring food," I said giving as clear a directive as I could.

I hung up the phone and mingled with the crowd. It became clear as I went in and out of the house that the food was going, going, gone very quickly. The group who just arrived would have little. I found a frozen soup in the freezer and brought it upstairs. Others were hungry, too. Should we order out — Chinese? Pizza?

Now there was music in the living room. Nicholas, who played violin at the funeral, was performing. Then someone played the piano. Music filled the house with a richness and softness that brought us all closer together. The language of music pierces through loss in a wondrous way, opening that which has been closed and bringing closure to that which has been torn open.

Some of the crowd began to drift away.

Beth was now in the back room with close friends in a more intimate setting. It was a more settled environment, and she was enjoying the mix of people who would gather in with her.

Finally, the cavalry arrived. Leslie and David came in with bags of food in their arms. I immediately surrendered the kitchen as they prepared simple hors d'oeuvres. Turkey and cheese sandwiches followed. With the hot soup, everyone had a nice meal.

They left shortly afterward. David had stayed up all night. He had had business in Chicago the previous day, had arrived very late at night, and then kept the vigil from 5 to 7 A.M. in Alison's room. We were grateful for their help. Leslie had displayed her strength through the preparation of nurturing food and had carried things off beautifully.

It was dark now and almost everyone had left. Still, people were arriving after work or with their families. The night went on lazily with an ever-dwindling group. At the end of the evening, Beth and I, the boys, Faith, Charity, Randy and Ryan, Adelyn, and Kay were all that remained.

We had decided that more is better, that to open up each day to all who wanted to participate would be best. Somehow, through the grace of God and the organizing power of caring people, what could never have been directed had come together on its own.

It was a long, grueling day with many hellos and good-byes and one very mighty and difficult good-bye. Yet the day had a good morning with preparations going smoothly, a good afternoon with a shower of love in a remarkable, powerful, and beautiful service, a good evening with friends, family, food, and intimacy, and yes, a good-bye, in a celebration of old and new rituals, spontaneity, and completion. More aptly, it was, "Adieu, Alison!" (To God, Alison!)

~

October 1995

Dear Beth,

Alison's death and your response to it were an extraordinary gift to me, my family, our school community and many many people you don't even know. I imagine your own experience of the last several days is burned in your memory with a bright clarity that will never fade, but I wanted you also to have the experience you provided others, as another way for you to see how powerful Alison was in her life and death, and how your instinctive, spontaneous actions were moments of grace for all who had the honor of knowing or being around you during this time.

I heard about Alison's accident early Monday morning when Cindy, whom I do not yet know, called in tears to tell me. Although we have not yet met, it was immediately a very intimate conversation, in which we connected through our love for you and our pain at the picture of your beautiful little girl on life support systems, getting acquainted with death.

Roger and I lost a little baby boy when he was three and a half months old. He had been more on my mind than usual for several days as his birthday approached, so as I talked with Cindy that time was very present to me. It touched me so deeply to connect with you at that time in a similar way. I shared some of that with Cindy and I felt so thankful to be alive and able to be intimate with strangers. We are all one, and we all suffer and love together, even when we pretend to be alone.

On Tuesday, my children and I visited the grave of my little boy on his birthday. I lay down on the grass and thought about you and Alison and my little boy and I felt an overwhelming love and peace and contentment, that even in the middle of this fire of sorrow is a cool calm place where our hearts can be safely broken open to the love that is all, everything. I fell asleep for a few minutes and woke up deeply refreshed.

The next day I went to our study group to be with other women and then to come to your house. The time was very sacred, very ancient, the weeping women, crying for you, for ourselves in your place, for our dear children so precious to us — how could we ever let one go? — for all the sad things, animals, people, everything that we love and don't want to lose. Over and over we heard someone say through her tears, "I just feel so bad for Beth." And in this way we bear each other's burdens, we cry each other's tears, because we simply could not physically do it alone.

Later we came to your house, which was already filled with flowers and food, the sacraments of human kindness. Your sweet mother was there, attentive to every detail including her own memories and sorrow. I went into Alison's room and cried for awhile, talked to her a bit, grew accustomed to her face. Your lovely boy Matthew came in. He showed me his bird, rearranged the toys in the casket a little, fussed over her. He just glowed. His wonderful smile. This wise, innocent man in a young boy's body. Other people came in. We stood together in silent weeping, and then slowly reached out and held each other's hands. A woman who seems like she hasn't cried since she was a little girl was wanting to be strong, but her hands gave her away — she was so fidgety, and when we took her hands she gave way, just gently, to her tears for you. You enabled so many people to move down into their hearts for a few days and to see what a Paradise awaits us there.

That afternoon I brought my children to see Alison. Jane had asked me to bring Kristen back and that turned out to be such a blessing, because Kristen made it very comfortable to see Alison. We spoke with you briefly, and you were very present, even though you had so much on your mind, you were totally there in the moment for us. Then I asked Kristen to lead us upstairs and she showed us the way, literally. My children were very quiet, but Kristen went straight to Alison's head and stood very close, very comfortably. My young son, Owen, took it all in and went from fear to horror to acceptance all in a few minutes. Alison's room was so beautiful he felt it was a safe place; after all, she had all these wonderful toys everywhere, it had to be okay. My daughter, Jesse, who is Alison's age, braided some onion grass. She took it around by Kristen to Alison's head, and very gently laid it across her breast, and then felt so loving that she stroked Alison's hands and face. Afterwards, my children went down and played on your trampoline, jumping, squealing, laughing and bouncing.

The next day was the funeral. The church was full when we got there and there were people standing in the back. When you walked to your seat, we knew we were in the presence of holiness. The hymns made everyone cry. They are such beautiful songs, such perfect words for a little girl's funeral! My children took it all in and when the high school chorus sang, I thought we had all joined Alison and were being greeted by the heavenly host. I felt they were singing from their Higher Selves out of the passion that is so painfully unique to teenagers.

Then we went over to your house for the reception. Tables had been set up on your lawn with freshly ironed tablecloths that did not match. They were not from a caterer. These belonged to people, maybe you, maybe your loved ones, and they had been taken out of a linen drawer, spread out with love to make everything beautiful. They were already covered with mounded plates of food and pitchers of drinks that glowed like huge gems. Nearby was a hand-carved wooden podium with the guest register on it, with colored pencils for children to make pictures if they wanted. Who brought those newly sharpened pencils? How did that podium get there? All the details, all the phone calls, all the willing hearts yearning to do something, anything to show you how much you are loved and supported. Let me bring some cups! I'll bake brownies! I'll be there early! I'll help clean up....

I stood on the porch and looked out at the scene. The late afternoon autumn sun was coming through the trees in that soft yellow-green light. The grass looked very soft. For some reason, many of the kids had taken off their shoes and were running around in their socks. People were streaming down the street, all carrying something — a grocery bag, a casserole, flowers. I looked at the people around the tables. There was a gentleness in the air. Our handsome young biology teacher was standing looking straight into the eyes of a taller, bearded man who was looking right back at him and talking quietly, and our teacher had tears streaming down his face. He did not move to wipe them away. He was so handsome, so radiant, so passionate. I walked through the crowd and my eyes met his. He smiled shyly, reached out, took my arm and said "How *are* you?" We had never spoken to each other before. I felt such love for him!

That evening, Roger's Canadian clients came to our house for dinner. I shared a little with them about the funeral. They listened closely, so I showed them Alison's picture that had been given out at the church. All the men choked up and couldn't talk for awhile. One of them took her picture back to Canada to share with his family.

I started writing this letter two days ago, and when I tried to print it, it seemed that the computer had eaten it. I started to cry, and prayed that I could not bear to lose the letter — I really wanted you to have it, and I could not write it again. I tried to intuit what I needed to do but neither the prayers nor the intuition brought forth the printed page. I had to leave to pick up my son, and as I drove I noticed my sickness at losing the letter. I backed off a little to get a better view, and then I saw: I had lost a letter; you had lost your daughter. How can such unbearable suffering be absorbed?

There is really no way to close this, because my love for you is open-ended. As they say, we are spiritual beings on a human journey, and now our roads are running close together. We are like two pilgrims on a gravelly path to some sacred site who find ourselves walking side by side. We'll share our water, some stories, long silences and attend to each other's wounds.

With love and affection,
Susie

out of the depths

THE DAY AFTER

Had anyone seen Pumpkin the kitty cat?

The day broke and we slept. When we awoke, it was not to the beauty that had been with us throughout the week but to an overcast somber day. It was cooler and looked ripe for rain.

Still the phone continued to ring. The school called. There would be a school assembly at 2:30 that afternoon. This was being held to bring closure for the students regarding Alison's passing. Would we like to come? I knew that the boys were going to Baltimore to see Rob at 4:00 P.M., and it did not seem possible. I thanked the caller and said that we could not come.

We went out for a late breakfast at a diner not far from the school. We ordered pancakes, French toast, eggs, sausage, bacon, the works. It was a fine time in a relaxed atmosphere and we enjoyed it immensely.

I had not mentioned to Beth that we had been invited to the school assembly. When I told Beth about it, she thought it would be worthwhile for us to attend. I called the school and said that we would be coming. Unfortunately, Kay had to catch her flight home, and Addie volunteered to take her to the airport. We said our good-byes to Kay and the eight of us piled into Beth's van for the short trip to the school.

We arrived late and as we went down the hall we passed the first grade classroom. There on Alison's desk were flowers and pictures and remembrances that the children had placed. The children's teacher had also made a large drawing on the chalk board of Alison as an angel traveling a beautiful rainbow back to heaven from earth. My heart caught in my throat, but we hurried on to the auditorium. The room was packed and everyone had been awaiting our arrival.

There was a hush as we entered and we made our way to the front row where seats had been reserved. A school administrator came to the front of the assembly. He read the following words spoken by Rudolf Steiner at the funeral of a Waldorf pupil in 1924:

> To lead you strongly into future life on earth,
> You were entrusted to our care by your parents.
>
> To speak with grief at the portal of death
> Is possible only by use of winged words of soul,
> Destined for your further ripening life.
>
> So take, in place of the school's past guidance
> For earthly deeds and life,
> The teachers' loving thoughts
> Yonder into that spirit-realm of being

Where the soul may be woven
Into eternity's clear, shining light
And where the spirit experiences
The aims of divine willing.

There was a short dance performance with a theme of resurrection and a song by the high school chorus. Nicholas, the violinist at the funeral, and another high school boy sang a duet, "Swing Low, Sweet Chariot."

A teacher came to the front of the auditorium. She had an allegorical story to share with the children. She began:

I want to tell you a story about a distant land in a time long ago. In this land there lived an Indian warrior who had done many heroic deeds and he would be chief one day. He was strong as a bear, fleet as a fox, and courageous as a mountain lion. He was in love with an Indian princess as bright and cheerful as a spring day. She was wise as the owl and watchful as the hawk circling high above. They were destined to be married and lead their people together.

The night before their wedding they went to their lodges to sleep. When the warrior awoke, he went to the lodge of the princess and found that she had died and gone to the top of the world where all spirits go. The warrior was heartbroken. He decided that he must follow her to the top of the world and bring her back to be with him. He set off on his journey. Everywhere he went, the Indian princess had already passed. Days stretched into weeks and still the brave continued on.

One day he came upon a lodge. An old man told him that he had seen the woman on her way to the top of the world. He told the brave that he could not catch her and that she would never return to his people with him. The warrior listened but he was determined to follow her.

The land slowly changed from green woods to brown prairie. The warrior continued day and night barely stopping for food and rest. Each day he traveled as far as he could go, always on the lookout that he might see her. Gradually the land became as though covered in a mist. It was as if it was not really land at all. He noticed that night and day became more like one another and that his shadow was very thin. He knew that he was almost at the top of the world.

Then, in that misty and shadowless world, he came to the edge of land. There was a large lake with land on a distant shore. It was the top of the world!

Out in the lake paddling hard, he saw the Indian princess. He grabbed a canoe by the shore and pushed off after her. He paddled so hard that his canoe flew like a bird across the water but no matter how hard he paddled, no matter how fast he went, he was not able to catch her. Finally, she reached land and was at the top of the world. Here, land, people, and sea were like the mist itself. The brave came on as hard as he could, paddling furiously for shore.

Suddenly, she shouted in a loud voice, "Come no further! I cannot go back with you!"

He yelled out, "I will not return without you."

"I cannot come," she replied. "This is my place now and I must remain here."

"I am coming to take you back with me!" he cried and he began making for shore again.

"Stop!" she shouted, "If you land here, you will never return to our people. Anyone who comes here must stay."

He looked at those on the shore and they were spirits. He looked at himself and saw that he too was becoming the mist.

"Our people need you," she said. "You must lead them."

He was quiet.

She grew thoughtful and then said, "I must remain here, but my spirit will always be with you. Call upon me and I will counsel you. I will be beside you. But now you must go. You are at the top of the world and nearly a spirit yourself!"

What she said was true and he slowly turned from shore. He paddled back across the great lake and returned to his land.

One day, not long after, he became chief of his people. Whenever he had a difficult decision to make or needed guidance, he would leave his duties and be by himself. Here, the bright and wise woman would appear to him and help him find what was best for the people. He lived to be an old man and was known as a wise and brave chief. He ruled his people with kindness and love and no one ever knew of this beautiful spirit.

One day, when his time had come to travel to the top of the world, he turned his power over to his son who now became chief. He told his son that whenever there were difficult decisions that he would be there in spirit to help his son guide the people. Then the wise chief made the journey to the top of the world where he was reunited with the Indian princess.

The assembly was beautifully done. Beth then asked to speak to the students. I watched her walk to the center of the room. Was she going to start to say something and then begin crying unable to finish? What was it that she wanted to say and share with this group of children assembled? She was in front of the first grade.

"I want to share a couple of stories about Alison with you," Beth began quietly and confidently.

"When we first began to have children, like many other parents, we had a book of names and what each name means. This helped us to find names that we liked. When I had my first child, we named him a name that meant 'Gift of God' — Matthew is his name. When our second child came we gave him a name that means 'Beloved' — his name is David. So, when our third child came we wanted to name her something that would go with our 'Gift of God' and 'Beloved.' We looked at a lot of names, but I kept coming back to Alison. It is a family name and was also the name of my best friend and neighbor when I was a child. So, we decided on Alison and when we went to look up its meaning, we found that it meant 'Warrior.' So Alison has always been our warrior."

Beth was connecting all that was important to her: family, spirituality, mission in life, the Waldorf school, and her personal philosophy. Her strong conviction was evident in her words. There was love pouring out of her. She reached inside and shared herself with these children, giving greater significance to this event in their lives.

"There is another story that I would like to tell about Alison," Beth continued. "Alison loved to dress up. Sometimes she would dress up in women's clothes and other times she would try to be scary. One of the things she loved to do was to dress up like a pirate. One day, however, she came upstairs from all of the play clothes dressed like an Indian. 'Oh, Alison you look so beautiful' I said to her. 'Are you an Indian princess?' She looked at me fiercely and said 'No', and then pointing at herself said, 'I'm the chief!!'"

The auditorium exploded in laughter at this story, especially those who knew Alison. The first-graders went wild. They were pretending that they were Indians with bows and arrows. The assembly came to an end, and we tried to leave to get the boys up to Baltimore to see Rob.

There was a great sense of family as we prepared to go. Many people were around us as we made our way out, sharing condolences and giving support. Fundamentally, people wanted to share something about this experience, not some "thing," but an expression that they were honored, inspired, and grateful to be part of this life-changing experience. It was pain, loss, love, and hope intertwined.

Again, we had been buoyed up, lifted high by the love and warmth of people who shared our experience and brought out their goodness to help ease our path. The harsh finality of the crematorium was softened by the wonderful flow of life in a school dedicated to the continuing mystery of self-discovery, a school in which Beth and her children were an integral part.

Once more, life had somehow overcome the despair of loss, and death had been cheated of the final victory. Death had won out over the body, but life had won the struggle over the heart and soul. In part, it was a dark time with flashes of light. More truthfully, it was a time of brilliant light with patches of difficult darkness.

October 19, 1995
Dear Beth and family,

It was quite extraordinary to see the love for Alison expressed by the second-graders. The little girls created a beautiful garden for her, and talked with me about how Alison could now play with them whenever they wanted. The little boys brought balls and treasures to her desk. They seemed to have a remarkably clear understanding that their friend has gone home to the angels.

We will miss Alison, here, very much.
Kindly, Martha

We dropped off Beth, Ryan, and Faith at Beth's house. Then Charity, Randy, Matthew, David, and I headed to Baltimore. Rob was still at Sheppard Pratt Psychiatric Hospital. At the facility, we came up a long driveway. There in front of us rose a large gothic building, forbidding and stark. We found our way inside and signed in. Then we went to the main entrance only to be redirected to another part of the building, then up an old staircase to a large locked door. We had a certain amount of concern in these unfamiliar and guarded premises. I waited outside; only family was allowed entry.

An hour later they emerged. Rob waved at me. He looked thin, gaunt, and unshaven, but he had vitality about him. When we got outside, I asked Charity how things went.

"When we got inside, we were taken to Rob's room because he is still being confined. The boys came to him and everyone had big hugs and kisses. After things settled down, Rob took both of the boys in his arms and said, 'We're going to have a long happy life together!'"

Lyn later told me that after the funeral, she and John, Rob's brother, had visited Rob. They had been uplifted by the service and were able to communicate this to Rob. Many people had asked about Rob and were praying for him, keeping him in their hearts. The day of the service had been one of closure, healing, and completion, and Rob was missed and needed in many ways. The love of family, friends, community, and well-wishers helped propel Rob forward, not just away from pain. Through his own "dark night of the soul" and from the support and love of others, Rob found the strength to pick himself up, with his wounds and his loss and his pain, and begin again.

Our spirits were high on the ride back to Washington, but we hit rush hour traffic. It was clear that Randy and Ryan would not make their flight home. We stopped en route and Randy changed their reservations to a flight the next morning.

We finally arrived at Beth's an hour later. We had dinner and enjoyed the quiet after the crush of so much activity. We all had a riotous time after dinner playing foosbal and stayed up very late. We were riding high from the school assembly and Rob's dramatic turnaround. It was nice to enjoy family and friends and live in the blessings of the moment. It was bittersweet, but the sweet made the bitter palatable.

TIMELESS

I tried for the longest time to teach Alison how to tell time. With the advent of digital clocks, reading a clock face is a skill that children often fall behind in.

Rob with David (left) and Matthew after a swim: Summer 1998.

Every time she would ask, "What time is it?" I would grab her, bring her over to an analogue clock and try to squeeze the answer out of her.

"Now, Alison," I would say, "where is the little hand?" and we would start a five-minute process of her zeroing in on the time.

It reached the point that when she innocently asked what time it was, she would immediately gasp knowing what would surely follow. I would whisk her up, and off to the nearest clock we would go. We had a couple of grueling sessions in the evening in front of the stove clock where I could manually move the clock hands. I would prop her up with her feet on the lower oven door handle so she was high enough to see the clock. I kept accidentally setting the timer off as I took her through her paces.

"Now, you see Alison — 'BZZZZZZ' — the little hand is at the three and the big hand — 'BZZZZZZZZ' — is over here at the seven and..."

It is not surprising that she had difficulty. Beth even bought a clock book to help Alison learn, yet on the whole it remained somewhat of a mystery to her.

Alison's time was spent being with others and improving life around her. She worked hard at understanding people and their needs. She did not work hard at lighting up a room, but she did that as well. That is what she had time for. She never did fully learn to tell time and, after she left us, I came up with a better plan that would have helped her learn.

The truth is that Alison had little time for things that she was not going to make use of in her visit to earth. She was not going to be with us long and there was no reason to count the minutes or hours. After all, time is relative and there is so much living to be done.

aftermath and going on

"The only cure for grief is love."
— Ioana Razi, MD (Alison's pediatrician)

Pumpkin the cat, whatever happened to Pumpkin the cat? Pumpkin was special, both independent and affectionate. He had been acquired two years before by Beth and the children on a visit to a farm in Vermont. They had no intention of getting a cat, but they all had been taken by this particular one.

He had been present at the house Tuesday, Wednesday, and Thursday amidst the turmoil and throngs of people (children!) but was nowhere to be found Friday when things settled down.

On Saturday and Sunday we looked for him and in the weeks ahead there was an all-out effort to locate him. We posted signs on telephone poles all over the neighborhood; we went looking for him up and down many streets far from Beth's house. The local Silver Spring paper did a human interest story about Alison and the lost cat in the hope that if anyone had information about him that they would contact us. We even turned to pet psychics who are "tuned in" to animals and can help locate them. Unfortunately, all of our efforts were to no avail and Pumpkin never reappeared.

One person divined that Pumpkin had left the house when the hearse went to the church, that he had followed it, not wanting to see Alison leave forever, and had traveled far from the house only to be taken in by a well-meaning stranger. It is noteworthy that the picture Beth chose for the Order of Service for the funeral was of Alison holding Pumpkin.

One time an orange tabby appeared in the backyard while Faith was home and she enticed the cat inside, receiving some scratches in the process, only to find that it was not Pumpkin. Beth and the boys had lost Alison, then they lost Pumpkin. It was not a huge loss, but it was a loss on top of loss. They have since gotten another cat, but there are always special qualities in a beloved pet that cannot be replaced.

ANGEL DANCE

The boys were allowed to stay home from school through the middle of the following week. One of the classes each of them takes is a movement class that integrates emotion and thought through physical movements. About a week after returning to school, Matthew had his movement class one afternoon. Beth was picking the children up from school that day, and when she arrived, Matthew's teacher came out as the children were loading up for the ride home.

"Beth," she said, "I just wanted to share something very sweet that happened in our class. We were doing a movement exercise where we pair off and there was an odd number of students. I was thinking of ways to work with the situation and Matthew said, 'I'll dance with Alison!' So I ran the exercise with the group and Matthew didn't have a partner. But it all worked out fine. It really touched me when he said that and I wanted to share it with you."

She smiled at Matthew seated in the back of the car. Matthew looked serious.

"Mommy," Matthew said, "I really did see Alison and I danced with her. She had wings and was a little older than before, but it was Alison."

Oh!

MEALS

Dinners were provided to Beth and her family for several months after Alison's accident. A sign-up sheet was posted at school. Many people, those who knew the family and those who did not, took turns providing nourishing meals and gave Beth a needed respite from preparing and cooking dinners.

ALL HALLOW'S EVE, OCTOBER 31

Halloween night, the boys got ready for trick-or-treating. Matthew, tall and thin for his age, went as the Grim Reaper. Art imitating life?

Alison's scarecrow finally had its day, sitting on the front stoop next to the jack-o-lanterns looking quite ugly and scary!

LIGHTING SNOWSTORM

On a Saturday evening at the beginning of November, a yearly All Souls celebration is held at the Washington Waldorf School. This is an opportunity to acknowledge all those who have passed on. Beth wanted to attend and asked Rob and Lyn to come down from Baltimore to join us. The boys' cousins were in town from Connecticut for the weekend, and they would enjoy time at home with them. My sister was able to baby-sit for Rob and Lyn's five-month-old baby, Lindsey. We decided to take Beth's van, and Faith and Beth's cousin Flip Turner joined us.

Rain started as we drove to the school. We arrived early and spent some quiet meditative time. The service was composed of readings, a beautiful movement performance, and music. The atmosphere was contemplative. Rob also had an opportunity to spend time with many friends he had not seen since the accident. The experience of the night was healing and positive, and we were glad that we attended.

Toward the end of the evening, the storm got worse and the wind picked up with a ferocious howl. By the time we got to our van, the temperature had dropped below freezing, the wind was roaring, and there was a heavy snowstorm. We drove home slowly. In the midst of it all, there were lightning flashes across the sky. None of us had ever seen anything like it — a lightning snowstorm!

We made it back to Beth's house over the slick roads, and Rob and Lyn decided it would be best to stay the night. We gathered in Beth's back room for hot and cold drinks with music on the stereo. The lightning snowstorm continued and we stayed up enjoying the novelty of the occasion.

Eventually everyone got to bed. Beth and I were in Alison's room. Rob, Lyn, and Lindsey were in Beth's room, and Faith, Flip, the boys, and their cousins were spread throughout the house. In a sense, it was unusual bedfellows, but more so, it was the harmony of a very extended family. The next morning there was a leisurely breakfast and quality time for everyone.

The All Souls ceremony was meant for contemplation and closure, and circumstances conspired to bring Alison's family together under one roof for a night. Normally, Rob, Lyn, and Lindsey would have gone home, but the magic of this night, and the forces of nature over which none of us have control, brought this group together as family for needed healing, companionship, and intimacy. It was also the first full night's sleep for Rob since the accident. This All Souls evening brought a unique experience and an unseen blessing for us all.

HOUSE GUESTS

Faith, Beth's mother, and Addie, her dear friend, stayed on at Beth's home for some months after the accident. They each helped with many needs, but more importantly, they brought themselves and their lives to share with Beth and the boys.

A friend would occasionally come by to play the piano. Alison had started piano lessons a few weeks before her crossing and the beauty of music again reverberated through the house.

Friends at school volunteered to clean and beautify Beth's house inside and out. A crew of women came several times and cleaned and shined, helping with whatever needed doing.

The house had lost some of its light in Alison's passing and the good will and love of friends and family brought back much of that luster.

꩜

November 13, 1995
Dear Beth,

It's hard to write since I have waited so long, yet I have many thoughts and feelings and a sense of connection with you.

I want you to know that I think of you and the boys daily. Having gone through the sudden death of my dad in a car accident when I was Matthew's age, I know that in many ways the hardest times are yet to come. As the intense focus on Alison's life and death dwindles, there is the sad reality of daily living with the huge hole she has left behind.

I feel so *with* you in this, yet awkward because I barely know you and I don't know how to share my support and connection to you. But I guess we can figure that out together.

With love and warmth,
Flora

In mid-November, about a month after the accident, Beth shared some of her experiences and feelings with me.

"Sometimes I feel that I want to die," she said. "Living with this loss is too much. No one should ever have to go through this. I just want to be with Alison. Life is so empty without her."

There was resignation and the understanding that she would never be the same. There was part of her that could not accept this and wanted to surrender to death, to give in and lose herself to what had taken Alison.

Beth developed an entirely new attitude toward death. She saw many people struggling to prolong life at any cost out of fear. She also experienced that life often meant hardship, sorrow, and strife. Alison had escaped all of that and perhaps had gotten the "big reward." Whatever afterlife there was for Alison must be a place of beauty and light. Beth, at times, wanted to go there, too, and escape this earthly struggle.

There was comprehension of the larger life of which we are all a part. In her own way, Beth had followed Alison to the "top of the world" and was seeing herself as both body and mist. She could never again view her life in the same way, and though the mist would recede, it had swallowed and changed the pattern of her life. Yet, Beth's mission, like the Indian warrior's, was to return to her family and responsibilities, and to live fully in the world. In this difficult transition, Beth hoped and prayed that Alison was with her on her journey, that through Beth's eyes and ears Alison could still be connected to earthly life, and that through Beth's actions, Alison's love and wisdom could continue to illuminate life's path and bring a ray of light into the darkness of this world.

Dear Beth,

You grew such a beautiful garden and your most delicate flower was taken. I'm so sorry and all my love and prayers go out to you.

May Alison merge with her true spirit and may her sweetness live on.

You are such a sweet and gentle spirit and it hurts to know the pain you have been given.

I know the strength of your spirit and the incredible love you have within you and surrounding you will carry you through.

Please let me know if you need anything — I am always here for you.

I love you, Shawna

Alison — Fly to your new home and take our love with you.

THANK YOU!

After the service and the week of activity at Beth's house, it took time for life to settle back into a pattern. Following on all of the events, there were many, many people to thank and acknowledge for their support during this overwhelming time: the hands-on help of organizing, the outpouring of love from the school, the support of family, and the love and support of many near and far. Beth thought of different ways to show her appreciation, and as Christmas was approaching and it would take time to print and address cards, we all thought that a combination Christmas card and thank you card was best.

For this, Beth wanted to use a picture of all three children. She had a good picture of the children from the summer before and we worked hard making everything right. Faith ordered three hundred cards and pictures to assemble and mail out. When we started to address them we found we were short. Altogether we mailed out six hundred cards to family, friends, and the families from the school! It took weeks in November and December to complete this project.

The quote in the card was from Sir James Barrie:

Those who bring sunshine
into the lives of others
cannot keep it from themselves.

Beth and the children's 1995 Christmas card. This note of appreciation brought together Christmas, thank you, and Alison in one eloquent statement.

Christmas 1995

Dearest Beth, Matthew and David,

Your beautiful Christmas card and letter brought tears. What a treasured moment and expression of the real meaning of this season, that each of us might have the gift of eternal life.

At this bittersweet time, may we reaffirm our feelings of love and friendship which have been a gift from Alison these past months.

May the joy of her glowing light burn brightly within you throughout the Christmas tide.

All our love,

Sheila and Todd Johns

CHRISTMAS 1995

With Christmas approaching and Alison's crossing still fresh, Beth was unsure as to how to spend the holidays. She did not want to do anything or go anywhere, yet a Christmas at home or in familiar surroundings seemed worse.

When the children were younger, Rob took them on a trip to Jamaica and the beauty and wonder of it stayed with them for years. Beth did not want to plan anything, but she felt that a change in scenery might be helpful. Her grandmother, who had recently moved to warmer climes, called with her condolences and asked Beth, the boys, and Faith to come spend some time with her. She helped arrange a trip over the holidays, and the boys were excited about traveling as well. I joined them and our trip to the warmth of the South was invigorating and healing.

Sometimes in the midst of grief it is hard to tell what might be helpful. Beth found that a change of environment, beautiful scenery, and peace and quiet brought the first glimmer of light in a long road of recovery.

THE BOYS

How are Matthew and David? How have the boys coped with the loss of their sister and changes in their family life? From all accounts including teachers, parents, and friends, Matthew and David are doing well. As children, their coping and recovery capabilities are strong. Their relationships with friends, their school work, and their participation in varied interests are all developing well. More than this, Beth feels that their home, school, and church environments all direct the boys to recognize a continuing life for Alison and the relationship that exists between herself and them. Beth encourages the boys to pray to Alison and to ask her for help and guidance. Although Alison is gone from their physical life, she continues to be an important part of their spiritual life and family.

Dear Sanders family,

I am a girl in the 8th grade. I just want you to know that I am sorry about your daughter, and sister.

My family knows how you all are feeling. My brother died when I was five and we all missed him very much but somehow got along in life without him. Just know that she was very happy the few years she was with you, and that you will meet again in another life.

Love, Shenbaga

GOLDEN THREADS

The nightmares that Beth experienced are gone. Their full import is impossible to determine. Like many difficulties in life, the nightmares served a positive purpose. About six months before Alison's accident, Beth had her first frightening nightmare regarding her children's welfare. She had a number of these dreams, the last being several weeks before the accident. When Beth had these dreams, she looked at how the loss of a child would affect her life.

Beth was given the opportunity to experience what it would be like to lose a child and then wake to the profound relief that that was not so. On a deep level these dreams heightened Beth's awareness of her children, the primacy of love, the gift of life, and, ultimately, what Beth can change and what she cannot. This served Beth in the loss of Alison — Beth lived consciously aware of each child's unique mission, vision, and path. Beth has lived through the most difficult loss for a parent, and she has done so with her children's good foremost in her mind.

Beth said, "The dreams brought a tremendous gift. Each time I awoke and found that they were not true, I felt that I had been blessed — escaped. Each day became precious, each exchange important, each moment wakeful and conscious of the tremendous privilege it was to guide, love, and care for these three lovely souls."

When Beth had her dreams, she felt that if any of her children died that she would need to go on medication for a year or more. It seemed that this was the only way that she would be able to get through the trauma. When the time actually came for Beth, no one approached her offering medication, nor did Beth seek any. Although Beth was devastated, she had a heightened experience, crystal clarity, and her mind, emotions, and senses were all highly attuned to providing care and support for Alison.

Everyone reacts differently to loss and Beth did what was natural for her. From conversations with friends and her own self-education, Beth understood that she could help shape the quality of her experience by being present to it. Although she could have asked for medication, she chose to go through this experience as consciously as possible. She also knew that, medicated or not, she had to begin her healing from the place of her loss. There could be no substitute for this internal emotional process and no amount of time could erase this need. She engaged herself fully and seized the opportunities at hand to make every aspect of the event as meaningful as possible.

When Beth had given birth to her children, she chose natural childbirth and had been awake and alert to the entire process. When Alison died, Beth chose a natural death process and was awake and alert there, too. She knew what she desired and with the advice of friends, she was able to choose the funeral arrangements and plans that were best for Alison, her family, and all involved.

Like natural childbirth, this simple act of natural death care has always existed, however, in this technological age, the benefits of hands-on involvement in life-and-death processes have become obscured. These benefits include co-creating our lives rather than being victims of circumstance, experiencing more completion in the comings and goings of our loved ones, and living consciously and passionately in the present.

This, of course, is a daily struggle for those who have had a great loss. Each person must find the combination of inner work and outer resources for healing when a life-changing event is experienced.

October 27, 1995

Dear Beth,

My heart has gone out to you and all your family in these last grievous days, in the dread time which all parents consciously or subconsciously fear.

During these days I've heard about your courage and inner embracing strength and about the many loving, supportive deeds of your friends. I've heard about your children's strength and confidence in Alison's now being both with the angels and with all of you and her friends.

Truly, the enormity of what this community has experienced through your dear Alison's seemingly untimely death can never be fully assessed, but it is clear that a little child is leading many, many people to a deeper and greater level of being.

It seems just as clear that Alison has mighty deeds to accomplish in the future, and she required but a short, vital earth life to make the last needed preparations. You and your family were and are her worthy aides, loving her wisely, allowing her to blossom, striving for her welfare, finding the right companions, schools and teachers, supporting her in her earthly death.

Yet I know also how now you will feel the questions, the anguish, the pain and weight of the physical loss of your beloved daughter with increasing heaviness, even while another part of you struggles for brave acceptance of Alison's individual destiny.

My heart with its thoughts of support and encouragement joins all those of others, dear friends and acquaintances, who silently support your soul. I hope that you will call on me.

With deepest sympathy,
Roberta

anniversaries and co-inkydinks

"Time doesn't heal all things, love does."
— Author Unknown

CO-INKYDINKS

In Beth's family, there is an expression for the word "coincidence" that the children used when they were little. The term is "co-inkydink." Here is a "co-inkydink" that occurred after Alison's passing.

JULY 27, 1996, ALISON'S EIGHTH BIRTHDAY

Rainy, drizzly, wet, cloudy, overcast, partly cloudy, sun breaking through, light rain, cloudiness, more sunshine — the beauty of being on a lovely mountaintop in the summer in Vermont.

By some twist of fate, Alison's Aunt Kay had picked Alison's birthday to be her wedding day. Actually, the day had picked her. Due to schedules with school and work, the availability of this wonderful mountain setting, and the minister's schedule, every date was eliminated except July 27. When asked how she felt about that day as Kay's wedding day, Beth said that Alison's birthday is a day for beautiful things.

We gathered on the mountain after much preparation by family and friends. It was a hands-on affair with work projects galore. Everyone had a chance to spend time together. Faith and her sister, Beth's aunt, put up their two families at a local bed-and-breakfast and there was ample opportunity for family time.

Kay opened the wedding ceremony by talking about Alison's special qualities and recognizing that it was her day as well. The wedding was beautiful. The view was breathtaking. Lake Champlain was below us and fields and hills stretched as far as the eye could see.

At the end of the ceremony, Kay invited all the children to the front in Alison's name. She invited Beth to come up as well. Kay gave each one a small paper packet. When the children opened the packets, monarch butterflies came forth to the "Oohs" and "Ahhs" of everyone. The butterfly in Beth's packet flew up and landed on her arm, reminding her of Alison's presence and surprising and delighting her.

After the ceremony, the sun emerged fully, and including a brief shower, it was a spectacular afternoon. There was a feeling of Alison in the air. There was some sadness for us but great joy in the coming together of family, friends, and new life, a man and a woman joined together in marriage. There had been a physical birth on that day eight years ago, now there was a spiritual birth.

The next day at brunch before everyone departed, Charity, Beth's life-long friend and cousin, announced her engagement. The date for the wedding would be October 19, the anniversary day of Alison's funeral. Again, it was the best date they could find. Was Someone up there trying to tell us something?

SUNDAY, OCTOBER 13, 1996

For the anniversary week of Alison's passing, Beth invited a group of women friends to attend a candlelight prayer circle at her home. This small event involved singing and was held in Alison's honor.

On the Monday of that week, Beth, Matthew, David, and I went hiking up Old Rag Mountain, a long hike up to beautiful views along Skyline Drive in Shenandoah National Park, Virginia. The boys and Alison had once done this hike with Rob. We took some of Alison's ashes with us. At the very top of the craggy mountain, we all took ashes in our hands. It was blustery though not cold.

Beth asked me to say a few words. I said a short prayer asking God to watch over Alison, asking for her guidance and nearness in our lives. I also recognized her love of people and nature as well as her universal spirit. Then we all said, "We love you Alison!" and threw her ashes in the wind, spreading them across the earth.

TUESDAY, OCTOBER 15, 1996

On October 15, 1996, the anniversary date of Alison's passing, the Waldorf School held an outdoor assembly in her honor. The school, with many helping hands, had created a beautiful memorial garden on Earth Day. Now was the perfect opportunity to come together at this garden.

It was a beautiful early fall day just like the year before. Rob, Lyn, and Lindsey were present as well as Matthew, David, Beth, and myself. Many parents gathered as well. The garden had many flowering plants and a few trees.

Songs were sung and there was a brief ceremony. There were small cloth prayer flags. Anyone who wished could write a note and then attach it to a tree branch in Alison's garden. It was simple and heartfelt.

Afterward, we gathered at Beth's house. Again, there was a great similarity to the year before, many children, great activity, delicious food, and wonderful friends were all present. We gathered in the dining room and kitchen before the meal. Beth asked everyone to keep Alison in their hearts and if there were any stories and memories of Alison to please share them.

We held hands and said grace together: "We thank the water, earth, and air, and all the helping powers they bear. We thank the people loving and good, who grow and cook our daily food, but most of all we thank the sun, the light and life of everyone. Blessings on the meal."

CO-INKYDINK TWO

On Saturday, October 19, 1996, the anniversary day of Alison's funeral, Beth's cousin Charity was married in one of the worst rain and wind storms in memory in southern Connecticut. The night before, at the rehearsal dinner, I said a few words about the occasion and that again life was springing forth from this loss. I also wished Charity and Rich blessings from Alison on their wedding day. The next day the wild weather was outdone only by the wedding reception and everyone enjoyed a terrific celebration.

Dear Beth,

I have never met you nor did I ever meet Alison, however, I want you to know how profoundly I have been moved by your lives.

When my mother was seven months pregnant with me she lost a child, her name was Dolores. (Dolores means sorrow in Spanish.) She got on the counter to get some crackers and her dress caught on fire from the stove. Her back was severely burned and she lived two weeks before dying. I was born shortly after and was given her name which I kept for forty-two years. At that time, I felt I wanted my own name and I changed it to Joy.

Throughout my life, I lived very much with the story of the other Dolores, mostly the pain and tragedy of her early passing. My mother lived with a profound sadness and my father never spoke of her. My brothers and sisters had little support in this because my parents were so paralyzed.

My son is in the second grade at the Waldorf School. When I learned of Alison's crossing, I was struck with a pain deep in my being and a grief that moved through my cells. I feel that a memory buried in me, passed to me while still inside my own mother, was awakened. I believe I mourned my own sister. With your willingness to share, and with a community so willing to be open, I feel as though I am reliving something from forty-seven years ago — for my mother and father, for my sisters and brothers — reliving now what couldn't be done then for all of my family.

I love you for your generosity of spirit and I pray for all of you.

I am deeply grateful to Alison for how she has helped me and I know she might connect with the other little girl who crossed long ago and still lives in my heart.

Sincerely,

Joy

legacies and silver linings

I believe that most of us come to this Earth to learn;
Wisdom borne of this life helps our souls transcend
to a place some call heaven.

Yet, there are people here on earth whose souls have
already transcended this life;

They enter it again not to learn but to teach.

I believe Alison was one of these people.

I pray that the ache in your hearts will soften and
that quiet reflection will reveal the wisdom she came to
share.

— Lurana

One of Alison's attributes was that she was a quick study. When she learned a new word or skill, she immediately began to use it with competency and ease. One evening Beth was reading the children a story before bed. They came across the word "beau" and the children needed an explanation. Beth described beau as a sweetheart or boyfriend. A few days later, Kristen's dad, John Parker, came to school at pick-up time with his longish hair and young features.

"Oh! That must be Kristen's mommy's beau," Alison said thoughtfully. Beth gave Alison a little more information, but she had gotten the idea!

Of greater significance, however, was Alison's ability to learn and integrate higher human behaviors.

When I first met Alison, I noticed that she had a natural inclination to help out and make others welcome. She did this spontaneously, but she was also nice because, "it was the right thing to do." One time, when she and Kristen were becoming good friends, she spent hours in the basement sawing and nailing, making presents at her woodworking bench. She gave a present to everyone in Kristen's family.

Later, I noticed that Alison had changed in her attitude of helping others. She had been rewarded for her helpfulness through smiles and special "thank yous," and she enjoyed this attention. Her earlier simplicity had vanished, and like most of us, the reward now created much of the motivation.

In the last year of her life I noticed that Alison's behavior changed once more. Alison was helping others because it genuinely pleased her to do so. The act of service created happiness both in and around her. Her joy was in the doing. She was still getting the accolades, but harmony naturally resulted for everyone. She was no longer being helpful because, "it was the right thing to do," nor because of the reward. Alison learned that her happiness could be multiplied when it was shared with others and that was reason enough to give of herself.

Alison did not live in a world where there was a loser for every winner. She had a clear purposefulness that was blended with an innate understanding of synergy. She lived in a world where life created from within itself and served life. Why settle for two when one plus one just might make three?

~

Dear Beth, Robert, Matthew, David, and all of Alison's family,

When I first met Alison as her movement teacher, she made such an impression on me — a kind of "Huckleberry Finn" child with no fear, someone who was really going to take on the world.

I remember thinking how great it is going to be to teach this young girl and watch her grow.

In our last movement class, Alison climbed the "rickety bridge" without touching a rod, and therefore earned her crown as a prince. Alison then went *back down* the rickety bridge to rescue her classmates.

Those classmates were waiting to be rescued, for they had unfortunately touched a rod and awakened the witch who had turned them into toads! However, if a prince were to successfully lead them back up the ladder, they would *also* become princes and princesses.

I remember Alison's burning eagerness to help and lead her classmates — and their love for her.

Alison has left us with a powerful gift of love and courage. I know it will inspire me and I thank her.

With love, Christina

S.O.M.E.

One night at bedtime, Alison spontaneously told Beth that she wanted to help the poor as her life's work. Alison was strongly affected when she saw the homeless or destitute and she always asked her parents to help them in some way. Beth wished to help Alison fulfill this goal, and when Beth was asked what people could do for her family at the time of the accident, she put a note in

Alison's obituary for donations to be made in Alison's name to S.O.M.E. "So Others Might Eat," a nonprofit group in the Washington, D.C. area that helps feed those who are not able to feed themselves. Many people made donations to this charity. Beth felt that she was just following through on Alison's inspiration.

In some ways, Alison's compassion, caring, and love brought greater blessings to others from beyond death than they did as a seed in a young girl's heart.

HIDDEN MESSAGES

Like other children, Alison did things that were endearing, wonderful, and individual. On weekends, when the children were with Rob, she would call Beth for various reasons, sometimes to complain, often to ask permission to do something, or she might call for a ruling on what the children were permitted to do. Usually Alison called just to say hello and to share her love with her mother. If Beth was not in, she would return home to find a message (sometimes two or three) on her answering machine.

As with many who have lost a loved one suddenly, there is a desire to preserve that person outwardly through what he or she has left behind. Weeks after Alison's passing, Beth, the boys, Faith, and I were discussing these calls and the messages Alison used to leave. Beth had often mentioned that she would like to save these messages. She wondered whether she had done this or whether there were any messages at the end of the answering machine tape.

I checked the answering machine by playing and fast forwarding through the tape. There were no messages from Alison. I turned the tape over and found this from the other side:

"Hello, Mommy, this is Alison and I just wanted to tell you that I really love you. I know I sended another message yesterday and you called me back, but I just wanted to say 'Hi' again. And I hope you're doing well, but I'll be back tonight. Have a good rest of the day. Bye. Remember, I love you."

Then almost as an afterthought, "And remember — this is Alison."

There were several other parts of messages. The theme was always, "Remember, I love you!"

ROB'S CRUSADE

Beth received a call from the National Highway Traffic Safety Administration a week after the accident and passed the caller on to me. John Knox's hypothesis about Alison's death and other seemingly related cases was gaining momentum and would eventually be proven. More data came in and the cause of Alison's death was known: she was struck and killed by the passenger air bag. The red scrape on her neck had been the result of the air bag inflating at nearly two hundred miles per hour and hitting her under the chin. The concussion had been so powerful that her brain had been dislodged in her skull and she had been killed instantaneously. Unfortunately, as in over one hundred similar cases of children and small adult deaths, there were not adequate warnings of dangers, nor was there *any* testing of air bags for children and adults of small stature. A great deal of suffering has been caused.

When Rob became aware that there were anomalies regarding the accident, he began to do his own research and found that certain auto makers use air bags that are especially dangerous. Other auto makers, mostly foreign, have excellent safety records and no air bag injuries or deaths. Recently, Rob's leadership and dogged determination prodded NHTSA to require safer air bag systems for future automobiles — a victory for every family. Still, for the safety of the public, NHTSA needs to release the list of cars with dangerous air bags and act strongly to have these air bags removed from the marketplace.

Rob brought Alison into that intersection, but the air bag killed her. Rob saw an opportunity to help others, bring meaningfulness to Alison's passing and, to a degree, vindicate himself in this accident from which his daughter should have walked away.

Rob formed Parents for Safer Air Bags, a nonprofit corporation that alerts the public to air bag dangers and promotes safer air bag design. He uses his legal expertise and has brought forth compelling evidence in this fight for child safety and consumer rights. He is tireless in his efforts and has certainly saved lives of children and shielded families from this needless tragedy.

REMEMBRANCES

In the guest book that was set out at the wake and funeral, there were many examples shared of Alison's thoughtfulness, helpfulness, and leadership qualities. She was admired by younger children whom she treated with great respect. She could wrestle with older girls and still hold her own. In her class, she helped teachers organize activities and took charge of managing her classmates. Also, she was always looking out for those less fortunate. After all, what's the good of being aware of others' needs if you can't make things better?

SILVER LINING

"There are times," Beth said almost two years after the accident, "when it feels that the fact that I even had a daughter is a dream. At other times, all of this, everything that went on here, seems to be a dream. I hate those times that I feel that I never had a daughter.

"Most of the time I feel that Alison is present to me and that the accident itself is the dream. Through my prayers, meditations, readings, and intentions, Alison is present in my life. It is as though she is upstairs sleeping or at a friend's house. I feel love and a deep connection to her, and I carry her with me as fully as I know how."

There are also the mourning tears, crying fits, and occasional screams from hell of a parent who has lost a child. There are times when there is a need to talk, times when the need is to emote, and many times when there is simply a craving for solitude and silence. There is the loss that cannot be measured.

Beth would give up all the good that has come forth from this accident, and much, much more, to have Alison back with her family, and there are still times that she would like to die and join Alison.

Both Beth and Rob have faced their own deaths in the death of Alison. Each of them had to make the choice for their own life to continue. Some days are better than others, some days are worse. Every day is a challenge.

However, Beth believes that Alison is in a place of light and love, and she looks forward to joining her there.

At the time of Alison's passing, Beth made conscious choices in the many decisions in front of her. These choices laid a foundation for Beth to continue with her life and to fully acknowledge that Alison has passed on. She has dreams about Alison and even in these dreams there is the comprehension that Alison is no longer physically present.

The most significant difference between Beth and many others who face unexpected loss is that Beth had friends who informed her of choices available to her. She had enough information to create what she most desired: to be with her daughter as much as possible in the ensuing days and to make that same opportunity available to her family, friends, and community. As a mother, Beth has always felt honor- and duty-bound to care for her children. Seeing this event through to completion was essential to her.

From the deepest level of her soul, Beth brought an awareness and beauty to Alison's passing. Beth was blessed with choice and there was a certain magic in that choice. There was magic in a community gathering at a home in support and love, and beauty in rituals such as the funeral service and the around-the-clock vigil. There was magic in what is nearly taboo in our culture, handling death, both physically and emotionally, in a direct and loving manner. There was magic and beauty in creating an environment for comprehending and experiencing the mysteries of life.

Beth was aware of what she wanted and created an experience that truly honored Alison. In Alison's death, wake, funeral, and cremation, there was grief and joy, loss and growth, silence and singing, and reflection and sharing. Living and dying stood side by side. At heart, Alison's journey is one of transformation, which has touched the lives of many.

Rob and Beth have chosen different ways in which to live their own transformations: Rob through grappling with air bag safety issues, auto makers, and lawmakers, and Beth by focusing on her connection with spirituality and her relationship to that part of Alison that can never die. She is also co-founder of Crossings: Caring for Our Own at Death, a nonprofit educational corporation providing information on choice at the time of death (see Appendix A). On different paths, Beth and Rob have found meaningful ways for this event to live through them.

At the time of the accident, Beth's relationship to Alison was foremost in her heart and mind. Beth had an inner clarity and outer resolve. She fulfilled this relationship both spiritually and physically by her care of Alison. Beth saw to Alison's every need right up until the end when she had to surrender her to the fire. She felt a responsibility for Alison's well-being that included body, mind, and soul, and was there as long as Alison needed care in any way. Beth did not want to delegate any of this care to strangers: she brought Alison into this world and she would escort her out as well. This experience has brought Beth peace and consolation. Also, by opening her home and her life to others, Beth allowed hundreds of people a similar participatory experience.

Those with children were greatly affected by Alison's passing. These included friends of the family and parents from the Waldorf School. Some knew Alison and the family well, others did not. In Alison's death, their worst fears were realized. Life is fragile and there is much beyond our control. Parents mourned Alison's death, Beth and Rob's loss, and the lives of their own children in an uncertain world. A lasting effect of this has been appreciation of children and the delicate, yet vital, role that parents play in their growth. More deeply, parents have experienced gratitude for their gifts in life.

In one sense, those gathered experienced that "There but for the Grace of God go I," and many people came together to face this storm. Ultimately, however, people joined together not because misery loves company, but because where two or more are gathered in the name of love, there is holiness and grace. In the darkness of that night, and in the trial of loss, the light of life shone simply and clearly, lighting the path and bringing warmth and companionship to all who gathered.

Alison's gift is the joining of hearts and hands in a connection that is both body and soul. It is a gift that transcends fear and inspires us through love to become co-creators in our continuing journey of spirit.

Alison's light shines brightly bringing illumination to many. You may know others who do so as well. I believe that they are examples to us, beacons for life beyond our limited sight. As such, they offer an invitation to us to live life fully and consciously — and go there too, through the grace of God.

A WING AND A PRAYER

One night, a few days after the funeral at bedtime, David was deeply upset at the loss of Alison. He appeared inconsolable and Beth's heart was breaking — breaking for her own loss and for the pain it was causing one of those dearest to her heart. She was in deep despair — all of the sadness of the world seemed to be flowing around her and she was at a loss as to how to comfort her child. Out of the depths of loss and sorrow, out of sheer desperation, she grasped the only thread she felt available to her at that moment.

She turned to both boys and said, "Let's say our evening prayers, and let's imagine that Alison is here with us, saying them with us as she always has. Imagine her sitting at the foot of your bed. Let's say our prayers with her, and let's say them for her since she can only say them quietly. At the end, we will tell her we love her. This is how we will say our prayers from now on."

So they began, and when they had finished, the despair was relieved and they miraculously felt comforted. The boys drifted off to sleep peacefully.

TO YOU, DEAR CHILD

Your light shone in our midst,
A candle lighting up the shadows of life
With joyous hope.
The candle in our home went out,
The light withdrew.
It will shine again to us
From the heavens.
The light will illumine our ways on earth
With love given and taken.
A star of hope will rise.

— Evelyn Francis Capel

THE BOY'S EVENING PRAYERS

From head to foot
I am made in the image of God.

From my heart right into my hands
I feel the breath of God.

When I speak with my mouth
I follow the will of God.

When I behold God everywhere,
in father, in mother, in all dear people, in
animals and flowers, in trees and stones,

Nothing can fill me with fear, but only with love
for all that is about me.

PSALM 121 (ADAPTED)

I look up into the hills whence cometh my help,

My help cometh from the Lord
who made heaven and earth.

He will not suffer my foot to slip.

He that keepeth me will not slumber nor sleep.

The Lord is my keeper and my shade.

He is beside me at my right hand.

"We love you Alison!"

epilogue

RITUALS AND RESOURCES FOR RENEWAL

Alison's Gift reveals the outcomes of the choices Beth made at the time of Alison's crossing from this life to life in spirit, choices that brought consolation and comfort in a time of intense pain and confusion.

When *Alison's Gift* is shared with others, people often ask, "How could you live through this?"

The answer, of course, is that you *can't* live through it. It can, however, live through you — and it does.

Life changes transform who we are. Birth and death are portals of life: physicality dominating who we are in the former, and spirit taking back our consciousness in the latter.

When death occurs, our loved ones can be honored and our grieving assuaged through how we choose to care for the body. Naturally, the body may not always be available to us, but knowing our options can help bring closure. Each of us has choice regarding our involvement when loved ones die. How we exercise that choice is up to us.

In the shock and disbelief of death, most of us allow our "undertaking" to be done by professionals. *Alison's Gift* shows that keeping our loved ones in the home can allow a death that is closer to what life was like with that person: we are able to continue to care for our loved ones, to tend to them, to minister to all the loving details, and to become acutely aware of the aspects of that relationship that we can choose *not* to lose. We also can clearly experience the finality of their earthly existence. All of this can be invaluable in saying goodbye to our loved ones.

We are blessed with meaningful medical options for our physical and emotional health when we know that we are approaching our last days on earth. We also have many resources for helping with grief and beginning to heal after the death of our loved ones. We are exercising more choice in these areas.

The final link is the time connecting the time of death and the time just after. There is little attention paid to the opportunities for closure at the time between death and burial or cremation. This is changing as individuals and families choose to take on some or all of the responsibilities at that time.

When death comes close to us, our world is shattered and we are left with only the shell of our loved ones to comfort us. No matter how prepared we are for death, there is always suddenness and shock. For those who die, the physical limitations of the earth are left behind and they have gone on to a new life. We experience our mortality and a piece of our world is thrown into the fire or buried in the earth with them. We mourn the void that they once filled and experience instability in having to re-create our lives. We see in the future the extinguishing of our own life. Our loss, although centered on our loved ones, is about us, and ultimately, we must create the closure and healing that will allow us to continue on. Mark Twain had an insightful view of this when he wrote, "Why is it that we rejoice at a birth and grieve at a funeral? It is because we are not the person involved."

When we view existence as concluding when we die, then death is the annihilation of everything. If, however, we view life as continuing in spirit, then our parameters for successful living change. It is noteworthy that the words for death in our society invariably focus on cessation of life (or are euphemisms for such.) Semantics reveal the crux of our difficulty with death: we define and experience death as "The End" and have no vocabulary for a process which at heart is spirit-in-transformation.

Our loved ones have embarked on a journey that we, in our own way, are forced to travel. Our path may not be of our choosing, but it is an opportunity for awakening.

Life will take everything it must from us to give us the self-discovery that we so desperately need. It has been said that God breaks our hearts so that He can enter them. As death takes us when we lose loved ones, so life also takes us, and we experience the full range of life from fear to love, from isolation to unity.

Most of us do not know what to expect at the end of life. Like children in the womb we are oblivious to the life we are in and the life we will be entering. Yet, the sole reason for the child's "world" or womb is to be a vehicle for entering into the larger life. Similarly, we have a blissfully ignorant view of our life on Mother Earth and the larger life that awaits us!

Fear of death (ours or our loved ones) is the most difficult fear to confront and all other fears melt before it. It is acknowledging mortality and releasing ourselves from the fountain and folly of youth. It is the final frontier we are inescapably drawn toward.

Many of us have given thought to our funerals and creating the atmosphere that we will die in, whether in the home or hospital.

However the actual time of our departing and its immediate effects upon the "undeparted" are largely ignored. In caring for our own, we face death and choose life. Here we have the opportunity to creatively and beautifully weave life into death and death into life.

Many people such as Quakers, Buddhists, Hindus, Christian Community believers, and Jews take an involved approach at the immediate time of death or have strong rituals for the first few days or weeks after death. Finding emotional closure through religious ritual or through rites of your own creation can be an important aspect in healing. Knowing your desires and choices will produce informed decisions that can be integrated into your lifestyle and background.

One of Beth's desires is to share with you the opportunity to create a meaningful experience in the reality of loss. For that reason she has established Crossings: Caring for Our Own at Death (information on the following page) and is dedicated to bringing light and love into this powerful and transformative area of living.

For those who decide to have a measure of direct involvement, an invaluable resource is *Caring for the Dead: Your Final Act of Love* by Lisa Carlson (Upper Access Books), a practical guide to state regulations that govern mortuary science throughout the United States that also provides general information on funeral arrangements from a consumer's point of view.

Another important resource is *Dealing Creatively with Death: A Manual of Death Education and Simple Burial* by Earnest Morgan (Zinn Communications), now in its fourteenth edition.

For spirituality to be alive in us, we must enliven it. We must re-form ourselves to challenges and opportunities in a way that is life-giving. This is the value of choice at the portal of departure: it can create conscious living and transform death from a fear-based experience and empty ritual to a healing ritual and an experience of love.

appendix a

Renewing Simplicity and Sanctity at the Transition Time of Death

CROSSINGS: Caring for Our Own at Death
P.O. Box 721
Silver Spring, MD 20918
Web site: www.crossings.net
E-mail: deathcrossings@msn.com
(301) 593-5451

Crossings is dedicated to the renewal of in-home after-death care. Our mission is to educate people about the value of caring for their own at death and to provide resources to make this experience as easy and rewarding as possible.

Crossings recognizes that both birth and death are significant for the individual, family, and community. Crossings' goal is to put the rewards of working with our dead back into our communities.

These rewards include:
- Empowerment — maintaining choice and honoring our dead.
- Tending to our departed loved ones.
- Recognizing our loved ones' ongoing journey of spirit.
- Bringing comfort and closure to ourselves at a time of grief.
- Embracing our own death and accepting our continued life in spirit.
- Saving money compared to the cost of a full-service funeral.

⁓

"The desire to have a death of one's own is becoming more and more rare. In a short time it will be as rare as a life of one's own."

– Rainer Maria Rilke

⋍

Crossings' resources include educational and inspirational materials. We offer pre-planning and at-need services that provide guidance in physical, emotional, spiritual, and legal matters. We are also developing seminars and workshops for in-depth knowledge and training.

As a nonprofit charitable corporation, Crossings will work with all who need our services regardless of their ability to pay. We are also dependent on your donations to provide valuable help to others.

⋍

Anyone who stays away from a death bed because of distress, because the physical aspects...can be so very unpleasant, will turn out to have missed the one experience of a lifetime which can make known the true heights of love.

– Evelyn Francis Capel

RESOURCE GUIDE

Dealing with death often begins long before physical cessation of life and continues long past burial or cremation. The time at death and just after death is a singular time for our healing and honoring our loved ones.

This resource guide is comprised of educational, inspirational, and practical tools for creating healing within our own lives and honoring the passage of our loved ones from this world to the next. It has been developed to provide choice in aspects of in-home after-death care. There is information on procedural aspects of dealing with our dead both legally and physically.

There is information on planning the arrangements for the death of a loved one or planning arrangements for the time of your own crossing.

The resource guide contains information on:

• What to do at the time of death. (Who to call, and who you need not call.)

- How to tend to our departed loved ones.
- What materials you will need, how to acquire them, and how to use them in step-by-step procedures.
- How your activities, thoughts, and prayers can support your loved ones as they cross from this world to the next. (The value of carrying your ones in your heart in the first days after death.)
- How to create a community to participate fully in this sacred event in your life. (How to talk about your plans and recruit family and friends to build a community of love and support for a crossing.)
- How to save money based on the cost of a full-service funeral. (In most states you can be the funeral director. In other cases, you can do some or most of the arrangements yourself.)
- What you can expect in caring for your own dead. (The experiences people have at the time of a crossing, what to expect in the days after death before burial cremation, the sights and sounds of in-home after-death care, experiences shared by others who have taken care of a loved one in their homes.)

The basic premise of Crossings: Caring for Our Own at Death is *that our souls are eternal* and that the work of tending to our loved ones at death has value both for ourselves and for them.

Historically, the family had the responsibility for the care of our dead. Over the last century this responsibility has been undertaken by professionals. Before this shift of responsibility away from families, caring for our dead was central to living and the various religions and nationalities that comprise our country had rich traditions for weaving death into the fabric of family and community life. The value of this experience has been lost as we have opted for convenience in the hectic pace of life. Yet, when death occurs, we are the ones who bear the loss and are left with an experience that can be dissatisfying and hollow.

This resource guide is designed to provide individuals and families with information on their rights to control this fundamental aspect of life and to bring the value of the sacred event of a crossing back into our family and community life.

This resource guide package includes:
- Our 50-page guide.
- Certain materials used at the time of a crossing: four yards of white silk, rose oil, lavender oil, cotton, and candles.
- A thirty-minute consultation with a Crossings representative is included (normally $30) for any questions or discussions that you would like to have.

Note: We ask that this consultation take place within thirty days of receipt of these materials to help orient you in their use.

RESOURCE GUIDE PACKAGE

The resource guide, crossing materials, and a 30-minute consultation cost $100.00; shipping and handling is $5.00; for a total of $105.00. Send your check to:

Crossings: Caring for Our Own at Death
P.O. Box 3158
Silver Spring, MD 20918-3158

CONSULTATIONS

Crossings: Caring for Our Own at Death offers telephone consultation for answering specific questions and helping you through decisions at the time of a crossing or in preparing for a crossing. Answers to other questions are covered in the *Crossings Resource Guide.* Our fee for consultation service is $15 per quarter-hour session or $60 per hour session. (This money is used to help cover our overhead and administrative costs.) The cost of the phone call is the responsibility of the caller. At this time we can only offer consultation services by appointment. Please call (301) 593-5451 and leave a message or e-mail us at deathcrossings@msn.com as to when you would like to have this service. We will call you back and arrange the best time with you.

SEMINARS AND WORKSHOPS

Crossings: Caring for Our Own at Death would like to know of your interest in seminars and workshops on caring for your own at death. We are researching nationally prominent speakers in after-death care and exploring the possibility of a seminar. We also want to offer hands-on workshops for working with the principles and procedures of caring for our own at death listed in the *Crossings Resource Guide.*

appendix b

WHAT DO YOU MEAN BY "CARING FOR OUR OWN"?

Caring for our own means honoring the crossing of our loved ones in their passage from this life. Generally, but not always, it means keeping your departed ones at home for up to a three-day transition period if they have died at home, or bringing them home for this time if they have died elsewhere. It means handling some or all of the care of the body yourself. This can also be done in conjunction with a funeral director and can include washing, dressing, and transportation of your loved one. Caring for our own means not using unnecessary invasive procedures on the bodies of our loved ones; it does mean creating an atmosphere conducive to the sacredness of their crossing.

AM I ALLOWED LEGALLY TO CARE FOR MY OWN LOVED ONES AFTER DEATH?

Almost all states allow you to care for own at death. Each state has its own regulations governing this matter. Depending upon the state, everything from transportation to final disposition may be within your power. To find applicable regulations, contact your state for laws and regulations governing the practice of mortuary science or purchase *Caring for the Dead* by Lisa Carlson (Upper Access Publishers), which had a newly revised edition as of September 1998. Lisa Carlson is president of the Funeral and Memorial Society of America. You can also contact us for general information.

IF I DECIDE TO CARE FOR MY OWN AT DEATH, DO I STILL CALL A FUNERAL HOME?

You do not have to contact a funeral director (unless the laws in your state require it). You can handle all the arrangements yourself with the help of family and friends. You will want help with transportation and other aspects of the process. Funeral homes charge a standard fee of up to $2,000 to respond to an initial request and for consultations as to arrangements. This does not include *any* services or materials such as preparation of the body, viewing or storage of the departed, caskets, and so forth.

There are times when a funeral director's services are necessary. We strongly recommend that you develop a relationship with a funeral director prior to needing specific services.

WHAT ABOUT EMBALMING?

We are often surprised to hear that many people think that embalming is required for the deceased. There are some situations where this is so, such as when out-of-state transportation is necessary. For the most part, however, embalming is *not* required and is undesirable due to the highly toxic chemicals used. Embalming only delays the breakdown of the body, it does not prevent this breakdown. It also denatures the body and artificially changes it at a time when peace and tender handling are most important.

HOW MIGHT CARING FOR MY OWN HELP ME IN THE ENORMITY OF MY LOSS?

No matter the circumstances of loss, we are never quite prepared emotionally. It always seems sudden. By having our departed loved ones at home, we maintain control in an event that is otherwise beyond our control. We are assured that our loved one is treated with the love they deserve. We feel less a victim of circumstance. We are allowed the time we need to assimilate this loss into our lives. There is greater opportunity for closure, and we are allowed ample time for an often difficult good-bye.

endnotes

Evelyn Francis Capel, "To You Dear Child," *Prayers and Verses for Contemplation,* Copyright 1992. Reprinted with permission of Floris Books, Edinburgh

Evelyn Francis Capel, *Understanding Death,* London, Temple Lodge Press, Copyright ©1979, Used in the Order of Service and Appendix A

Alfred Lord Tennyson, *Poems*, "Charge of the Light Brigade," 1894

ORDERING INFORMATION

FOR MORE COPIES OF *ALISON'S GIFT*:

TO ORDER BY MAIL (CHECK OR MONEY ORDER):
NOSILA Publishing
P.O. Box 3158
Silver Spring MD 20918-3158

TO ORDER BY CREDIT CARD (EXPEDITED SERVICE AVAILABLE):
Big Books from Small Presses: Upper Access Books
(800) 356-9315

Alison's Gift costs $16.95 plus $3.00 shipping and handling.
(There is no additional S&H for orders of two or more books.)
We ship most orders the day they are received.

FOR THE CROSSINGS CARE RESOURCE PACKAGE
OR TO MAKE AN APPOINTMENT TO SPEAK WITH
A CROSSINGS CARE REPRESENTATIVE:

Crossings: Caring for Our Own at Death
P.O. Box 721
Silver Spring, MD 20918-721
(301) 593-5451

The Crossings Care Package consists of our 50-page guide, the
materials used for a crossing (Silk, Essential Oils, Candles, and
Cotton), plus a 30-minute Crossings Care Consultation. The cost
is $100 plus $5 shipping and handling, for a total of $105.
TO ORDER, SEND A CHECK OR MONEY ORDER FOR $105 TO
CROSSINGS.

ADDITIONAL INFORMATION:

Parents for Safer Air Bags
1250 24th Street N.W.
Suite 300
Washington D.C. 20037
(202) 467-8300 Fax: (202) 466-3079
Robert C. Sanders, Director and General Counsel